# Tales of One-who-seeks

by
Colin Berg

Illustrated by Ginny Westland

Calligraphy by Ginny Jarrett

Schofield Publishing Co.
29928 Lilac Road
Valley Center, California 92082

Library of Congress Catalog Card Number: 83-061415
First Edition 1983

ISBN 0-9608720-1-9

# Acknowledgments

*I would like to express my gratitude to the following people for their contributions to the production of this book: Ted Bear and Caroline Blakemore, editing the manuscript; Buck Bierly assisting in the typesetting and layout; Ginny Westland, illustrating the story; Elizabeth Berg, patience and support for a preoccupied husband during the months of writing; and Ginny Jarrett, project coordinator.*

*Thank you all.*
*C.B.*

This book is lovingly dedicated
to my teachers,
for their gifts;
and
to my students,
for their promise;
with the hope that in
finding the Way,
we may also
enjoy the journey.

# TABLE OF CONTENTS

# THE PREPARATION

# THE CHRISTENING

Singer-Of-Silences, a Teacher in the ways of power, loved to walk in his garden early every morning before his students returned from their nights' journeys. One morning, as he moved along a particularly beautiful place in the path, the Teacher came upon a small boy peering intently into the shadows beside the way.

"What is it you seek?" the man asked.

Startled, the boy whirled around, his face becoming at first very white, and then, very red. Apology, explanation, defense, and apology again were in desperate competition among themselves to be first out, so the poor boy was left mumbling unintelligibly. Mortified, the youth managed only to bring an even deeper color into his face, and then, unable to bear more, fled down the path stumbling headlong more than once in his haste to be away.

Some days later, Singer-Of-Silences was again walking in his garden, when coming upon a shady pool and an inviting expanse of long grasses, he decided to pause in order to listen to these, his soft-spoken neighbors. The Teacher had barely settled himself and opened his senses to enjoy this quiet interchange, when he did indeed hear a great deal, but of a nature not in tune with his anticipation.

There was considerable rustling of leaves and branches: louder than squirrel, rabbit, or hen; less purposeful than the larger inhabitants of the place. Suspecting the source, and not wanting to create greater havoc than had been already expressed, Singer-Of-Silences began to hum softly, allowing the melody to drift in the direction of the intruder. Immediately the rustling stopped. And then, more slowly, it began again, this time interrupted periodically by a short whistle, as if beckoning to someone or something.

Shortly, the bushes on the other side of the little pool moved, and out stepped the same young boy who had found speaking so difficult a few days earlier.

"I was looking . . . for my dog!" the boy said, looking around him with wide blue eyes at everything but the direct gaze of the Teacher.

"What is the dog's name?" asked Singer-Of-Silences.

At this the boy blushed, and without another word, slipped back into the wood. In a few moments the sounds of running footsteps faded into stillness, and Singer-Of-Silences was left to resume his conversation with the garden.

For several weeks thereafter as he took his morning walks, the Teacher caught glimpses of the boy: slipping behind a tree to hide; kneeling, unaware of observing eyes, at a quiet pool; and once, curled among the roots of a large tree with the light of dreams playing upon his sleeping face. Singer-Of-Silences did nothing to attract or frighten away the boy, but simply watched, and waited. It was not uncommon for people to find their way into the garden, but most wandered out again when their curiosity was appeased by brief exploration. It was unusual that one so young should come into the place, and then so persistently return; and so it was that Singer-Of-Silences found his own curiosity piqued by the tenacious, if timid, young explorer.

As the Teacher came round a curve in the path one bright morning, he found himself face-to-face with the boy, who now stood in the middle of the road, his widespread feet planted firmly and his arms crossed on his breast as he glared at the man before him.

"Who are you anyway, that you try to run me out of here? I have as much right to be here as you! I haven't been doing anything wrong, so why should you care if I poke around in some old garden?"

Finishing this lengthy speech, he took a deep breath, set his jaw tight, and glared as fiercely as possible into the eyes of Singer-Of-Silences. What he met there, however, was other than what he had expected.

The Teacher's unflinching eyes looked right back into the boy's, and before that silent, piercing gaze, the carefully rehearsed belligerence faltered, and then broke. The boy's whole body drooped, and despite the lowered head, Singer-Of-Silences could see tears on the young face. Again the youth spoke, but now just over a whisper.

"Please tell me, what is this place? Ever since I found a small entrance, I can't stay away. It frightens my mother when I tell her, but she doesn't understand that here in this garden I feel like I am supposed to be here, and nowhere else. Something pulls me here, and I can't find it. Please, let me stay. I won't hurt anything."

At these words, the Teacher's eyes, too, glistened. And in the stillness that had settled between them, he spoke.

"It is I you seek; for as keeper of this garden, I hold the keys that may unlock the doors of your understanding. This place is an entry and exit point on the paths of power. If you remain, and follow in the ways of the Teacher, the Healer, and the Warrior, much will be asked of you, but only because much will be given to you. The keys to the kingdom of life will be within your grasp, and with them you may find all that you now seek."

With every word the boy's eyes grew larger, his stance taller; and when Singer-Of-Silences had finished, he clutched the Teacher's hand, and promising to return, ran to gather his belongings and to bid his mother and father good-bye. Soon he returned, so flushed with excitement and exertion, that Singer-Of-Silences gave him his first lesson in the ways of power.

"There is within you a secret place, a garden whose pathways lie waiting for your touch. Sit quietly now, and I will show you how to find this sanctuary, for its secret will become your guide, and your most precious possession as you move along the paths of power. A seeker's finest tool is his awareness, and it is in your inner garden that you will be able to gather your awareness together, and lift it into an enlightened focus. In this way, you will bring the very best in you into each experience and event, and you will be able to see, know, and understand the meaning within each lesson."

After some time, he beckoned to the boy to rise, and the two returned along the garden path. As they walked the Teacher spoke of some of the journeys that lay ahead. When they came to the Halls of Learning, and passed through the great doorway, Singer-Of-Silences turned to the Keeper of Records, and pointing to his companion said,

"His name is One-Who-Seeks."

# THE PATHS OF POWER

Singer-Of-Silences had just welcomed a group of new students to the challenges of the ways of power. As he looked out across the gathering of young and old faces, he recognized and smiled at the boy he had recently met in the garden, One-Who-Seeks. The Teacher then became more specific in his talk, as he outlined for the students the focus of the training they would receive over the next several years.

"The ways of power are infinite in the nuances of their expression, and we do not attempt to either limit those expressions into one true path, or include within our teaching every possible means of travel. It is our goal to prepare you, through disciplined training, so that as the nuance of expression that has been chosen to bring power uniquely through you is revealed, you will be ready, able, and willing to carry that power outward with clarity, purpose, and joy.

"In order to realize that goal, we have focused the training in three primary areas: the Teacher, the Healer, and the Warrior paths of power. As you will soon see, these three interrelate very closely, so that a master of one must also function well within the others. As students, you will learn the basis of the art within all of them. As time goes on, you will then be able to refine your training in one or possibly two of the systems, according to your particular gifts.

"Your first exposure will be to the Teaching path. It is here that you will learn to move inwardly in order to draw the power outward. You will learn to unveil that which is already present within you, waiting for your ability to respond, to match its ability to express. This is the basis for all subsequent training, for without the experience of the internal Infinite, no Healer could touch, no Warrior could move, with hope for success.

"On the Healing path, you will learn to restore the integrity and vitality inherent within all life-forms to the abundant levels of their true design. It is often thought that healing is the repairing of wounds. This is true, but there are wounds of mind, and of identity, as well as of the body. Each must stand interdependently integrated with the others—healthy, responsive—in order for the Spirit, the Infinite, to achieve and maintain its full expression. The Healer's art is one of subtlety and finesse, for the restoring and maintenance of balance among widely disparate forces is a delicate maneuver. His is the ability to restore the ability to respond.

"The Warrior path is the art of application. Here you will learn to move throughout the whole dominion of your nature, and by the power of your active presence, insure the quality of your existence. Once the Teaching path has revealed to you the power within, once the Healing path has reawakened your ability to respond to that power, then you must know what to *do* with that power. In this, you will need the Warrior's art. Whether you truly become a fully robed Warrior, and undertake the missions he is given to accomplish, or go another way, you will need his art. It is on the Warrior path that you will learn to stand inviolate within the goodness, beauty, and truth of your own special gifts. Only in this way will you be able to receive fully, and give fully of those gifts.

"There is much to do before the garden, which is our beleaguered world, may bloom again. We are both its gardeners and the seeds which will bear its finest fruit; so tend this life and your living with care that our harvest might be most bountiful."

# THE LESSONS OF BALANCE AND ALIGNMENT

"There are two lessons that above all others you must learn and master if you aspire to the ways of power."

Singer-Of-Silences was again speaking to One-Who-Seeks and the other new students, and all sat in their best stillness as the Teacher continued.

"If you were to learn nothing else and yet master these, you might possibly have learned all; for within the lessons of balance and alignment, the very essence of life and the keys to its expression exist.

"It is difficult to say accurately that these are two separate lessons, for in truth, balance and alignment are the same force, applied along two different planes. They are companions, and for the seeker, inseparable.

"Balance is your relationship with your outer environment. It is the horizontal guide to your goal. As you find the skill and develop the art of maintaining harmony from yourself outward, and from outward back to yourself, you will find the joy of effortless motion.

"In seeking balance, observe the animal kingdom. They move not apart from the rest, but as one part of the one whole. The remarkable facility of movement demonstrated by some species is due in large part to their relationship with their environment—their ability to *adapt and move,* based on what they find in their environment.

"For human beings, it is much the same. Balance is not simply a physical skill. Rather, it is an attitude that expresses as upright posture and grace of mobility within the physical body, as well as within our thoughts and ideas, our feelings and emotional relationships, and our sensory perceptions and perspectives.

"The major difference between us and the other life-forms is that we have the ability to add dimension to our balance: alignment is your relationship with your inner environment. It is the vertical guide to your goal.

"The key to understanding and experiencing alignment is to realize that all form has a vertical axis that aligns it with the Infinite. In order for you to find the power of the Infinite, and then be able to move along its paths, you must learn to keep the purity of that alignment intact; for it is along the axis that you may invoke that power, and from the axis that the Infinite will express its power.

"As you find the skill and develop the art of maintaining the impeccability of your alignment, you will find the boundless joy of effortless internal motion, as the Infinite and the finite within you move as two, intermingling; and merge as one, interhabiting.

"I have said that balance and alignment are one force applied twice; that they are, for the seeker on the paths of power, inseparable. Perhaps this story will dramatize for you the truth of this statement, and the need for you to embrace it in your understanding.

"Three men undertook a long journey together. One was a great hunter, famous for his physical prowess and balance. One was a great holy man, renowned for his wisdom and alignment with the Infinite. One was neither famous for his balance, nor renowned for his alignment, yet as you will see, he possessed both.

"As the three went along their way, it was decided that each should contribute to the group's success according to his own particular gifts. Thus, the hunter procured the meat to sustain them; the holy man chose the wisest paths to follow; and the third saw to it that all the various parts cohered as a harmonious whole.

"This last was no easy task, for the hunter, unaccustomed to traveling with men unskilled in the ways of the wood, found himself overextending his companions' endurance. He was a man who considered himself fearless, for he knew that he could function as well as anything he would see. Alone, he loved the excitement of challenging survival, but with these others, he was not able to proceed with the abandon that his balance normally afforded him.

"The holy man, in turn, presented other challenges. Unaccustomed as he was to emerge from his contemplative life, he knew little of practical things. Finely attuned to the Infinite, he was sadly discordant with the finite. He could see and travel great distances internally, perceiving truth and falsehood as it lay about him. Because of this, he knew not the fear of the unknown. But neither did he know how to travel one foot after the other.

"For many days this trio walked through the countryside, encountering adventures here and there, but generally proceeding smoothly toward their end. Then, as light began to fade one day, a fog rose up and obscured their path, and within minutes they were separated from each other.

"Luckily, they all were able to grope along in the right direction. Since the hunter moved the fastest, he reached a clearing in the fog before the others, and there before him lay a sight that gave his normally brave heart pause. It was a ravine so filled with fog, it was impossible to determine its depth. Across this ravine, as a bridge, was a single, narrow plank.

"Suddenly fearful of the prospect of falling off the bridge into an abyss of unknown depth, the man hesitated. Yet, knowing his path lay forward, and that his lost companions may already be waiting for him on the other side, the hunter stepped onto the plank, and

slowly made his way across. However, as he reached the middle, fear took hold of his legs, the balance that had been his pride deserted him, and the hunter plunged into the foggy chasm.

"Shortly after, the holy man emerged from the fog and stood at the edge of the gully. With his inner sight, he perceived that its depth was only a few feet, and so without a second thought, he blithely proceeded to cross. Fear could find no hold on this man, but then, fear was not needed. Strength and coordination were in such poor supply that shortly after he had begun, the holy man pitched over the side of the bridge into the waiting fog.

"Finally the third man found his way to the little bridge. Pausing, the man sensed that no real danger presented itself here. From all the indications of his sentience, the fog covered a very shallow ravine; and he knew he was capable of crossing over the plank. Thus, he too stepped onto the bridge, and in moments was safely on the other side. Once there, he decided that it would be wise for him to wait for his companions, or for the fog to clear.

"He did not have long to wait for either. In a matter of a few minutes, the ravine that had been so obscured by cloud was quite visible. And there, firmly ensconced in the mud, were the hunter and the holy man: uninjured, but exceedingly embarrassed."

Looking deliberately into the eyes of each of the students, Singer-Of-Silences continued.

"Therefore, align your balance with the Infinite, that you might know the unknown, and move with ease through it; and balance your alignment to the finite, that you might know the joy of standing, as well as the joy of understanding."

# HUMILITY AND TIMIDITY

"How can it be that a Warrior must move humbly along his way, while all manner of fools may strut and swagger as they pitch headlong through oblivion?"

One-Who-Seeks had been among a group of young students who had that morning witnessed a remarkable demonstration of the Warrior's art by one of the teaching masters. At the close of the demonstration, the master had spoken of the need for the student to take special care in the cultivation of the Warrior's attitude—in relationship with his world. One of the most important qualities to develop, he said, was humility. Without it, no one could hope to truly walk the paths of power.

This seemed in direct opposition to the demonstration he had just witnessed, and One-Who-Seeks, afire with enthusiasm to learn and master the art, was not yet ready to understand or accept the words. In turmoil, he had left the demonstration, and after some time had sought out his Teacher, Singer-Of-Silences. It was to his mentor that he was now expressing his confusion and frustration.

"Surely if anyone has a right to some show of pride, it is the Warrior. Humility seems a denial of the power he is there to serve. How can he stand upright in his duty while timidly asking permission to pass? He should *declare* his presence, not apologize for it!"

A smile flickered in the eyes of the Teacher at these strong words from the young boy, but he also knew they came out of an honest, if ignorant, love for the subject. Therefore, he neither laughed at, nor rebuked the presumption. Rather, he made a seemingly very strange request of the student.

"Do you know the old man who sits outside the gates of the city? Go to him, give him this coin, and wait. You may sometimes find your answers where you least expect them."

One-Who-Seeks did indeed know the man. It was he who had for many years been the victim of much ridicule from the city dwellers. The boy himself, when in the company of friends, had teased the man, and laughed as loudly as the others at "the old fool." However, there had always been an air about this "fool" that had kept One-Who-Seeks from ever attempting to approach him alone.

So it was that as he went off on this peculiar mission, the boy found his heart pounding, and his mind racing for excuses not to continue. However, he soon reached the gates of the city, and there, just beyond, sat the old man.

Taking a deep breath, One-Who-Seeks walked quickly up to him, placed the coin Singer-Of-Silences had given him where it could be clearly seen, and stiffly sat down. For several minutes, no word passed between the two. It seemed as if the old man was unaware of the boy's presence. But then, looking with surprisingly blue eyes directly at One-Who-Seeks, he said,

"Humility comes when a man knows the source of power, and understands his small but vital part in its expression. Timidity is the act of one who neither knows the source, nor understands that he may find it. With the latter, a man either passes meekly underfoot without a sound; or boasting loudly, stumbles headlong over his silent companions. With the former, a man may enjoy his journey, for he suffers neither from the fear of weakness, the inability to do anything, nor the fear of strength, the responsibility to do everything. He knows the joy of being part of a whole larger than his sums. He needn't declare his presence, for his Presence declares

him."

On his way back into the city, One-Who-Seeks saw the Warrior-master who had given the demonstration and the accompanying talk on attitude. Running up to the man, the boy described his experiences throughout the day: his excitement at the demonstration; his indignation at the lesson; his conversation with Singer-Of-Silences; and his visit to the old man. Impulsively, One-Who-Seeks then bowed to the master in the traditional formal acknowledgment of a teacher by a student.

"I am now ready to listen, as well as eager to learn."

Returning the bow with equal formality and grace, the master spoke,

"You are now ready to learn, One-Who-Seeks."

# THE ART OF MAKING WHERE YOU ARE
## THE PERFECT PLACE TO BE

One-Who-Seeks woke excited and alert. In fact, he had been in such a state most of the night, even in his dreams. This day was to mark the beginning of his physical training in the Warrior's art. Up until now, the focus of the lessons had been on theory, and on cultivating the appropriate attitude. This was fine, as One-Who-Seeks had said to one of his fellow students yesterday. For awhile. But now he could begin the *real* training, and the youth's eagerness was proving a severe test to his fledgling balance and alignment.

Normally graceful and composed in his morning preparations, One-Who-Seeks found himself dropping and tripping over objects as he made ready to leave for this important day's lessons. Finally, laughing at himself, he went back to the first lesson in the ways of power that Singer-Of-Silences had taught him; and sitting down, gathered, enlightened, and focused his awareness, bringing the power of his eagerness into a more controlled expression of enthusiasm. Thus prepared, One-Who-Seeks went in search of his dream— to learn and master the way of the Warrior.

The Warrior-teacher was waiting as One-Who-Seeks and his companions arrived for their lesson, and when all had gathered, he welcomed them, and began by saying,

"As you know, we will begin the physical aspects of your Warrior training today. The first step in that training is to learn the ceremonial Warrior dance. This dance has many names, but for now, we will call it the Art of Making Where You Are the Perfect Place To Be.

"Most people live their lives, figuratively and sometimes physically, rushing past where they are, in their hurry to get where they're going, or where they'd rather be. A Warrior can't afford to do this. In order for him to accomplish his missions, he must make full use of every moment given to him. Therefore, he resides where he finds himself, and trusts that by performing here with as near to perfection as is possible, he will be preparing the way for each successive step. Otherwise, he lands blindly from moment to moment, and must spend much of his time reconnoitering his position, rather than performing his task.

"The first outstanding quality of the dance that you will notice is its tempo. It is very slow. This represents the Warrior's care and devotion to perfection at all times. Understanding that the eternity of life is as present now as it will be tomorrow, he is satisfied with the moment of eternity presently his to enjoy.

"Also, the slowness of the dance, coupled with its high degree of complex precision, forces you, the student, to keep your racing, impatient mind in harmony with your pedestrian and placid body. The steps together weave a tapestry through the dance, each step a stitch that leads to the next, until, reaching the end, you have woven a seamless garment of motion and light—a precursor of the Warrior robes you may someday wear.

"Do not think that because this is your first training tool, it is somehow inferior to those you will come to know and use later. The Art of Making Where You Are the Perfect Place To Be embraces everything else, and is the foundation upon which all your subsequent Warrior training will be built. Just as the beauty, strength, and endurance of a magnificent building are dependent on its foundation for their existence, so the future Warrior skills you develop are all dependent on your learning and mastering of this dance. Come then, if you would be Warriors."

Here, the teacher led his students onto an open field and guided them through their next steps in the journey toward mastering the ways of power. One-Who-Seeks was astonished that learning the dance involved relearning the act of walking itself; or rather, learning to turn the act into the art of walking. This, it seemed to him, was the essence of the dance: that any and every act could be art, given the proper respect and attention.

One-Who-Seeks loved the dance from the start. For although he felt clumsy and frustrated many times in the beginning, he knew intuitively that he had found his place. As he practiced his steps, gaining greater and greater proficiency and power, he recalled the teacher's words.

"There are four basic principles to keep in mind and body while practicing the Art of Making Where You Are the Perfect Place To Be. First, your foundation is in your feet. You cannot expect to maintain balance with your environment, and alignment to the Infinite as you move, if you do not balance and align the building of your body on the foundation of your feet. By your relationship to earth, in the way you move upon it, you will demonstrate the Warrior's way. As your feet are your connection to the earth, it is here that you will rediscover the love for life, and the commitment to your Warrior tasks. This is the internal foundation that allows you to build and maintain the attitude of joy in fulfilling your purpose.

"Second, your power is in your thighs. Do not let the weight of the world settle on your shoulders, and so propel you forward by the sheer force of that mass in motion. If you do, your feet will be left to scurry after, as your head heedlessly hurries on, without foundation. It is much wiser, easier, and more powerful to stand over your feet, and sinking in your knees, allow the deep power of your legs to send you gliding through space. In this way, you have greater choice in where and how you land.

"Third, your control is in your waist. Do not wander rudderless along the path, allowing your middle to dip and sway off your axis to the Infinite. A small movement here goes a long way. Therefore, temper your motion with wisdom, that it might ripple out gently and pervasively.

"Fourth, your expression is in your hands. Much of what is spoken is done so without words. Let these silent songs be sung with your hands as you dance, for there is much joy, as well as great beauty here. But remember too that your hands must remain attuned to your foundation, your power, and your control. Else, they are nothing but the pretty wavings of winds.

"You have choice in your living. You may, as many do, pass, unseeing, great portions of countryside as you run to reach your goal. But in whatever manner you proceed, remember the lesson of this dance, so that in pursuing your destination, you do not pass by your destiny."

# THE POWER OF ONE AND
# THE STRENGTH OF MANY

Feet-Of-Mountains-Hands-Of-Cloud, the master Warrior-teacher, brought several of his advanced pupils into a novice class one day to give some of the younger students a demonstration of power versus strength. Directing his guests to line up opposite him a few yards away, the teacher placed a large ball several feet high between himself and the group of students. Then, turning to his beginning pupils, he explained the nature of the demonstration.

As representatives of massive strength, the group of advanced students was to rush forward and attempt to push the ball across a line a few feet behind the teacher. As representative of single-pointed power, Feet-Of-Mountains-Hands-Of-Cloud was to resist the students' drive, and attempt to force the ball across a line some feet behind where they now stood.

Then, to further dramatize his point, the teacher invited any of the young observers to join the advanced students in their attempt to overcome the single resistance he was to make. One-Who-Seeks, who was a member of the novice class, stood up and volunteered to add his growing strength to the combined forces of the students. He did not quite understand why his teacher was so determined to fail, but as is often the case with students and their teachers, he relished the idea of winning against Feet-Of-Mountains-Hands-Of-Cloud—especially when the odds were so one-sided. The whole demonstration seemed to embody the quiet arrogance that the student had come to associate with his teacher, and which he now found unbearably offensive.

So it was an eager One-Who-Seeks, the glint of anticipated victory in his eye, who lined up opposite Feet-Of-Mountains-Hands-Of-Cloud, and waited the signal to begin. At a word from the master, the group of students rushed toward the ball, fully intending to force it across the designated line, and willing to sacrifice the dignity of their teacher should he be foolhardy enough to stand in their way.

As all this developed, Feet-Of-Mountains-Hands-Of-Cloud stood quietly with his arms crossed upon his breast. Then, as the students began to gain momentum in their charge, he sank in his knees, lifted his hands, and turned them palm-outward to face the rapidly approaching forces.

Immediately their progress ceased. In surprise, many of them, including One-Who-Seeks, stumbled and fell to the ground. Taking one step forward, Feet-Of-Mountains-Hands-Of-Cloud pushed out with his hands, sending the remaining students sprawling and the ball flying back across the line that had been drawn behind the students before they started.

As the advanced students gathered themselves up, they were laughing among themselves, because even though they had wholeheartedly entered into the spirit of the demonstration, they knew what the result would be—they had seen it many times before. However, for the observing novices, it was truly an amazing experience. Most of them sat wide-eyed and speechless for several minutes, and then began to talk excitedly among themselves. One-Who-Seeks was stunned, and more than a little embarrassed. He had been so sure of the outcome, and now to have been so wrong!

As the class departed, he approached the master to apologize for not trusting his ability, and for seeking to humiliate him with defeat. Feet-Of-Mountains-Hands-Of-Cloud listened quietly to the student's embarrassed contrition, and then smiling into One-Who-Seeks' eyes, invited him to take a short journey with him into the countryside.

During the course of their walk, One-Who-Seeks expressed his confusion and amazement how one person, even a master Warrior, could withstand the gathered forces of so many at once. Speaking into the student's ears with words, and into his mind with meaning, the teacher began to explain some of the basic principles of the way of the Warrior, and how in following this path, one began to experience things outside the realm of the usual and the common.

In this fashion they traveled several hours, and not a few miles, when, approaching a village in the late afternoon, they saw a large crowd milling around some point of focus, yelling and brandishing their fists in growing agitation. Slowly, teacher and student came up to the crowd, and as they drew close they saw the object of its anger.

It was a traveling huckster of a kind common to that area, who had (according to one of the local villagers standing next to the two newcomers) sold a great deal of special herbs and potions that he promised would do all manner of special things. Unfortunately for him, he had been delayed in his departure because of repair to his wagon, so that now he faced the wrath of a populace who had found his goods to be less than that. They were, in fact, useless.

Having been made to look and feel foolish, the people were in no mood for reasoning or compassion. They intended to exact payment for their financial and emotional discomfort, with his physical pain. If he managed to survive their "collection," he could count himself a lucky man. If not, well then he was simply reaping his just harvest. It was into such a state of outrage that the villagers had worked themselves, and it was obvious that if something wasn't done quickly, their outrage would soon spill into outrageous action.

Admonishing One-Who-Seeks to remain safely apart from the crowd, Feet-Of-Mountains-Hands-Of-Cloud slipped into the swelling mob, and began to work his way among the villagers, humming softly to himself and pausing now and then to say a few words to a neighbor. After some time, he had passed back and forth through the crowd several times, and as he went, the volatile mood began to quiet and settle, so that in a few more minutes, what had been growing into an ugly roar, diminished to a disgruntled murmur.

Now was the most delicate moment, for unless some satisfactory solution could be revealed, the crowd would once again explode into fury. Feet-Of-Mountains-Hands-Of-Cloud stood among the leaders of the group—those gathered directly in front of the accused huckster. Without a word he stood among them and waited. Finally, one of the leaders spoke.

With an edge of disgust still in his voice, he declared that this poor excuse of a man wasn't worth the time and energy they were wasting. Walking up to the cringing man, he demanded that all of the money he had taken from the villagers be returned, and that he never show himself in their region again. Although this meant the loss of considerable financial gain, the huckster was delighted to be rid of the place with any part of him still intact. Quickly he handed over the money, gathered up his belongings, and left.

The leader who had spoken now set about returning the money to those people who had lost it. When this was done, the crowd began to disperse, and in minutes, the street was empty save for Feet-Of-Mountains-Hands-Of-Cloud, and an admiring One-Who-Seeks.

As they continued on their way to search for a place to spend the night, the master resumed his speaking of the Warrior path.

"Remember, One-Who-Seeks, it is not the *form* that counts. It is the *stance* within the form that is important. If you rely on strength, speed, or technique, your success will always be dependent on your only meeting adversaries of inferior strength, speed, and technique. This is not the way of the true Warrior.

"If you would meet success in your journeys, wherever they may lead you, you must rely on the secrets of your own inner power. When you hold the stance of that power inviolate, you are truly a force to be reckoned with. Then, whatever action or apparent inaction you take, it will be effective. This is the art of the Warrior. Study it well."

# A MISSED OPPORTUNITY

One day, a teacher of One-Who-Seeks was walking along the road when he saw the young student lying asleep under a tree. Thinking this would be a good opportunity to offer him his next lesson, the teacher went over and sat down beside the youth, waiting for him to return from his slumber.

After some time, however, it became apparent that One-Who-Seeks was determined to stay asleep. And so the teacher rose and went on his way, finding another student who was awake, and ready for the lesson of the day.

# STANDING-IN-MUSCLES-LIVING-IN-BONES

Feet-Of-Mountains-Hands-Of-Cloud was giving One-Who-Seeks and several other students a lesson in the art of being a Warrior. This day, he had chosen to speak to them in a parable, and this is the story he told.

"Standing-In-Muscles-Living-In-Bones liked to think of himself as a simple man. Not simple-minded, but unencumbered by the multitude of needs that ambitious taste creates. As a boy, he had entered a training school in the ways of power, and so had received the name that, to his thinking, was to become more curse than the intended blessing.

"He was a gifted student, and his teachers were pleased with the promise he showed, but there was about him an undisciplined air that caused them some concern. Therefore, when his name was to be chosen, his naming Teacher presented the young student with one that had great power, but that would require his growing into it.

"This was a gift that was also a test. However, in his youthful impetuosity, Standing-In-Muscles-Living-In-Bones saw only the test, and resented the name. Shortly after this, he left the school to pursue his studies alone.

"For many years he read and traveled extensively, seeking to answer the imprint he bore—the need to know the nature and purpose of power, and his place in its expression. He acquired the lifestyle and habits of seekers he had seen, honing the focus of his living into a narrow blade of existence.

"But always in the distant background was a mild discomfort, an

unspoken doubt in his direction. And then there was the constant reminder of his name. Standing-In-Muscles-Living-In-Bones. Did not the name itself convey ambivalence? It was true that carrying a power name accorded him some status in the world, and he was honest enough to admit that he enjoyed this small pleasure. But he chafed at the gnawing fear that the name was a description of his inclination to be at odds within himself—being one thing, and doing another.

"As he grew older, he came to brood on the meaning of his name, and at such times would subject himself to the most painful of self-examinations. It was in such a moment of dark recrimination, the shadow of discontent wrapped about his fine features, that Standing-In-Muscles-Living-In-Bones approached the outskirts of a large city. He had just been thinking that 'Standing-In-Muscles' represented his youth, and the early training he had received in the ways of power. This was his potential. 'Living-In-Bones' he saw as representing what he had become—a prematurely aged ascetic; a man who sought the source by emulating form, but who eschewed involving function.

"Thus finding a certain perverse satisfaction in analyzing and acknowledging his 'failure in life', the man came to the gates of the city. As he drew close, an old guard seemingly far past the age of such work caught his eye, for the man was dramatically shaking a gnarled finger and a tenuously supported head in the direction of the traveler.

" 'Standing in muscles, living in bones, you are,' crowed the old man.

" 'I *am* Standing-In-Muscles-Living-In-Bones. But how do you know my name?' demanded the younger.

" 'Name? I know no name for you. I only know what you are, and that's plain to see. Standing in muscles, living in bones. I've seen your kind before, on the road into the city. Always with the same look in the eyes—that searching forward for something that were better found in the direction from where you came.'

" 'Who *are* you, old man? I tell you, my name *is* Standing-In-Muscles-Living-In-Bones, but no man has ever spoken aloud *what* I am. I am in great doubt of that myself.'

" 'You say your *name* is Standing-In-Muscles-Living-In-Bones? What sort of fool do you think I am? You expect me to believe that a power name of that sort would be given to the likes of you?'

"As he spoke, the old man's voice rose higher and higher, until at this last, it broke off entirely. And then, with an ease surprising for his apparent age, the man snatched up his staff, leaped to his feet, and stalked off.

"Standing-In-Muscles-Living-In-Bones was left stunned and immobile. He remained at the gate into the evening until finally, cold and hungry, he entered the city to find lodgings and the comfort of a warm meal. For several days he stayed there, and as he walked the streets examining the shops and all the places of interest, his mind returned to the old guard at the gate; and from there, to all the places he had seen and choices he had made since leaving the training school of power many years before.

"As he reminisced, Standing-In-Muscles-Living-In-Bones swore softly to himself, 'What a fool I have been!' However, he did not this time indulge in harangues, but determined to set out on the long journey back to the school to seek permission to resume his studies.

"For reasons not entirely clear to himself, Standing-In-Muscles-Living-In-Bones felt compelled to seek out the old man, and tell him of his plans. Unable to find him at the gate and not knowing where else to look, he turned to the innkeeper for assistance. However, when Standing-In-Muscles-Living-In-Bones asked the man and described the guard to him, he shook his head firmly.

" 'There is no guard of that description at that gate. In fact, at this time of year, no one needs guard that gate. For years now, during this season, it has been the acknowledged "territory" of a great Teacher and man of power, Standing-In-Bones-Living-In-Muscles. It surprises me you have not heard of him, for as he left our city today he asked of you, and left this for you.'

"At this, the innkeeper produced a small packet and, handing it to the other, went back about his business. More than a little amazed by all this, and with his curosity now fully aroused, Standing-In-Muscles-Living-In-Bones eagerly opened the packet and read the letter inside.

" 'My son,

Never seek to emulate a *form*, simply because power has expressed through that form in someone else. The power in another is theirs alone—and so the form they build to house that power must also be unique to them.

Stand in your muscles, for in you that is where the power lies. Once you have found that power, and the two of you have embraced and come to terms, you may learn to live with power throughout all your varied systems, even into your bones. That is a treasure worthy to be found.

But seek first your power seat. Finding it, stand in it. And from that seat, you and your power will move from the softest fluid muscle, to the hardest crystalline bone, as living testimony of the Warrior's way, and its ability to express in any guise, at any time.

In anticipation of your further growth toward that end, and the possibility of sharing experiences along the journey, I am,

Standing-In-Bones-Living-In-Muscles.'

"That day marked the beginning of his long-awaited return to the ways of power, and Standing-In-Muscles-Living-In-Bones, destined to become one of the greatest Warriors and Teachers of his time, set off eagerly, like a child reborn."

# THE GATHERING OF SEASON'S LAST FRUIT

The farmers in the region where One-Who-Seeks lived had a custom that had been handed down through so many generations, no one remembered when or how it originated. It was simply part of their way of life. In this custom, the last week of harvest came to be known as the Gathering of Season's Last Fruit.

As in all farming regions this was a time of great activity, but with an additional emphasis: each family drew a portion of their yield aside, and divided this portion again. With the first, smaller part, they prepared a small feast for the members of their family. With the second, larger part, they helped prepare a huge feast for all in the region. These feasts were part of the festival of the Gathering of Season's Last Fruit.

In their celebration of the festival, people toasted the fruits of their labors, and expressed their thanks for the abundance before them. If their yield had been great, their essence was great. If their yield had been small, their essence was accordingly small (though great in *quality*). It was a time for examining time spent; and accepting responsibility for results.

The seekers on the paths of power had adopted this custom, and adapted it to their particular pursuits. Acknowledging that the ebbs and flows of energy that the planet underwent in its cycles of fertility were also present within themselves, they set times for activity/action, and times for activity/rest. In the Gathering of Season's Last Fruit, they would bring to focus all the experiences and lessons they had had in their active time, examining and acknowledging progress made, and areas where growth was still needed. This time saw the cessation of most class studies, as teachers and students withdrew momentarily within themselves for a personal evaluation and recognition.

Then, in a group celebration they would gather together in a festival of their own—demonstrating the new levels of training and art they had achieved; the new techniques they had discovered; new ideas they wished to explore. It was a time of great joy and excitement, with singing and dancing playing a vital part in the proceedings.

Also at this time, advanced students who were ready to don the lighted robes of their chosen path were presented to the assembled companions. In a ceremony filled with mystical wonder and delight, they were given the Teacher, the Healer, or the Warrior robes they had earned. This marked a new and major step in their journey, for they were now acknowledged as standing singly illuminated—no longer a charge under the power and light of their Teacher. After receiving their robes, these people again withdrew—waiting for wisdom to reveal the direction of their next steps along their path.

One-Who-Seeks was not yet among this group of students, but he was to receive public acknowledgment and ceremonial gifts. He was part of the group ready to accept their apprentice cloak. This, too, was an important step, for it opened many doors to adventure and growth. For One-Who-Seeks, putting on the Warrior-apprentice cloak meant that he would soon be sent on his first missions: initially with partners, under supervision; and later alone. As he grew, these missions would grow in importance and responsibility.

As he stepped onto the dais to receive this acknowledgment of past growth and future promise, Singer-Of-Silences and Feet-Of-Mountains-Hands-Of-Cloud rose to meet him. It was the master

Warrior-teacher who placed the cloak round One-Who-Seeks' shoulders, and the master Teacher, Singer-Of-Silences, who spoke.

"You have traveled far, One-Who-Seeks, since that morning in my garden when caught in your attempt to find the answers to its secrets, you could not speak, but only fled down the path from where you came.

"I am delighted that you chose to return. May the wisdom that guided you to that choice continue to guide you along the way. There are many lights within you as yet still veiled; and many darknesses around us that wait for your unveiling. Carry on then, as you have begun; and we, your companions, will hold you ever in the light of the goodness, beauty, and truth that promises to come."

# JOYOUS-LAUGHTER-GENTLE-TEARS

One-Who-Seeks was on his first solo mission as an apprentice. Ever since activity had resumed after the Gathering of Season's Last Fruit, the young man had pursued relentlessly his goal—the mastering of the Warrior's art. Because of this he had progressed quickly, but Feet-Of-Mountains-Hands-Of-Cloud was concerned, for in the course of his plunge forward, One-Who-Seeks had fallen into a common trap of young and committed students. Taking his goal seriously, as he must to reach it, the youth had taken on the seriousness that is deadly to the pleasure and joy that may also be found in learning the ways of power. His commitment was becoming obsession, and it was this that had led the master Warrior-teacher to approach Ear-To-The-Infinite-Eye-To-The-Song for assistance.

The master Healer listened carefully as his friend spoke.

"One-Who-Seeks is a gifted student at a critical junction in his journey. He has demonstrated remarkable facility for the Warrior's art, but in focusing toward his goal, he has lost the peripheral perspective that allows him to laugh. As you know, my friend, humor is not only a vital part of the Healer's art. It is indispensable for the Warrior, for he could not long stand under the weight of his tasks and accomplishments without it. One-Who-Seeks' fixation on his end has locked him rigidly into one stance, one nature. He will need all of himself to reach the end he so earnestly pursues. So I am seeking your help in restoring his ability to respond with joy to all that lies ahead of him.

Ear-To-The-Infinite-Eye-To-The-Song smiled. "I, too, have a student in need of special care. It seems that each might serve to aid the other.

"Joyous-Laughter-Gentle-Tears is herself a Healer of no small art, though still a young student. She is particularly skilled in healing wounds of identity as you have described in One-Who-Seeks. However, she is continually overtaxing her capacity to heal herself, for she has not done well in her Warrior training. It is not for lack of ability, but she does not think of herself as a Warrior, and so does not practice the art. She has been out on a healing tour, and is now waiting for a guide to bring her home. I had hoped to send her to you, that you might speak to her about the applications of the Warrior's path, but perhaps One-Who-Seeks could perform that task."

Feet-Of-Mountains-Hands-Of-Cloud agreed. "Sometimes the best teacher is a fellow student."

Thus it was that One-Who-Seeks found himself on his way to a nearby village to find the young Healer-apprentice, Joyous-Laughter-Gentle-Tears. It was common that as those learning to walk the Healer's path began to go out on their missions, young Warrior-students would serve as their guide, and so further their training as well. One-Who-Seeks had gone on such missions before, but only under supervision. With the freedom of traveling alone —himself now the guide—he was more excited than he had been since receiving his apprentice cloak. As he moved on, he thought of Feet-Of-Mountains-Hands-Of-Cloud, and the words he had spoken as One-Who-Seeks prepared to leave.

"Do not overextend yourself as you go, One-Who-Seeks. And be doubly careful of this as you return. You will have the safety of another as your responsibility—one who does not know the secrets of endurance as you do. But do not mistake unfamiliarity with ignorance. This is a special student you go to meet, and it is a special student who goes to meet her. If both listen, both may learn much."

One-Who-Seeks smiled, recalling this. He did not know that this approaching meeting had for long years lain waiting to happen; that this young girl was to play a vital part in his journey, and he in hers; that she was to become his confidant, his companion, his beloved. He simply smiled, and continued on his way.

Several days later, Feet-Of-Mountains-Hands-Of-Cloud and Ear-To-The-Infinite-Eye-To-The-Song were walking together, when they came upon the two young people. One-Who-Seeks was showing the girl the basic power stances and steps in the Art of Making Where You Are the Perfect Place To Be. In their easy familiarity and their frequent laughter, it was apparent that the two found pleasure in what they did.

"It seems One-Who-Seeks has found Joyous-Laughter-Gentle-Tears," remarked the master Healer.

"And that she has found her teacher," laughed his friend.

# THE PRINCIPLES OF UNISON, HARMONY, AND DISCORD

One-Who-Seeks had a fellow student who was his arch-rival. In everything these two did, they tried to outdo the other. When they were young, this served to extend their capacities, and enabled them to progress more quickly. Thus, their teachers watched in silence as the two young competitors vied for excellence.

However, as they grew older and more sophisticated, the rivalry between One-Who-Seeks and Silent-Runner became more serious, as they sought less to excel than to prevent the other from excelling. When alternative styles of training were offered, these two always chose opposites. In discussions they always took opposing views and dominated all others with the intensity of their exchanges.

They were, in fact, very like each other in temperament, but differed greatly in their talents. Because there was a strong affinity between them, they sought each other's company and strove to impress the other. But with their fields of excellence so widely divergent, they had from the start fallen easily into the trap of competing *against* each other—each to prove that his own was the superior way.

Their relationship had become more and more demanding of their energy, while less and less productive of beneficial results. Finally, after the two had exploded in the middle of a lesson disrupting the entire group, Singer-Of-Silences called them into his quarters and issued a stern rebuke.

"Your teachers have been more than patient with your behavior. We had hoped that as you grew older and more adept in the ways of power, you would release your need for this childish one-up-manship. Instead, it would appear that your personal competition has become more important to you than your further growth, and the stability of your relationship with your other companions.

"You have damaged the harmony of the group, and so you will be held responsible for its healing. Until you prove your willingness and ability to move beyond this behavior pattern, you cannot be seriously considered as ready to move into new levels of training.

"However, both you, Silent-Runner, and you, One-Who-Seeks, have in all other areas demonstrated great potential and considerable art, and I know it is within you to succeed. Do not waste further time in doing so.

"To aid in the completion of your task, I have arranged for you to attend a lesson with the music-master. His class awaits you now."

Baffled by this last, and humbled by the whole experience, the young men went to find Cool-Breeze-Morning's-Song, the music-master. They soon came upon him and a small group of students seated under a large tree. The master smiled as they approached, and beckoned for them to be seated. Then, turning his attention to all of the assembled young people, he spoke.

"The lessons for today are the principles of unison, harmony, and discord. Master these, and you will have mastered much, for the art of song and of the dance were naught, if not for these three.

"Unison has two or more voices singing the same tone, or an octave of that tone. This is the simplest relationship in design, and yet perhaps the most difficult in expression. It is very rare to find two strong voices who will agree on one tone—this takes tremendous discipline, demanding much of each. Therefore, in your songs and dances, seek not unison in every one lest you become too easily discouraged, and leave off singing and dancing altogether. There is great power in this form, but it is not for everyone, every time. Learn its secrets, and you will be satisfied.

"Harmony is the most complex relationship in design, but once learned, can be one of the easiest and most pleasant in expression. In this, two or more voices sing different tones, but tones that have been mutually agreed upon, and found to be compatible. In this way, the strengths of many voices can be used to great advantage without sacrificing either individual taste, or overall beauty. The discipline required here is diplomacy, so that you may find the best series of tones for the voices involved. This is not always easy, but its result is one that most will find desirable; and in these cases desire is a worthy ally. Study this form well, and you will never want for companionship.

"Discord is neither complex in design, nor difficult in expression. It is, however, difficult to tolerate in any but the smallest amounts. Here, two or more voices sing different tones incompatible with each other. The voices, in effect, vie against each other for supremacy; wreaking havoc not only on the ears, but on the entire sensory environment of the audience. This is highly effective for attracting attention; but because of the adverse emotional content in this kind of attention, it is unwise to indulge in discord except under the most controlled circumstances. Learn this form's lesson quickly, lest you have to digest slowly its unpleasant fruit."

One-Who-Seeks and Silent-Runner looked at each other, blushed, and then burst into laughter. Startled, the music students turned and stared at the two. However, Cool-Breeze-Morning's-Song simply smiled, his eyes twinkling. Leaping to their feet, One-Who-Seeks and Silent-Runner thanked the master for their lesson, then,

bidding the class farewell, ran off into the distance.

Many times after that, even into their old age, these two friends were called upon by the Warrior council to be sent on missions and adventures to the farthest outposts on the paths of power; for rarely did two voices blend so clearly in a mutual understanding and appreciation of each other's gifts.

# WHEN TO BE A WARRIOR

One-Who Seeks and some of his companions were engaged in an animated discussion on the subtleties of pursuing the paths of power. The group had recently been initiated into a new level of their training, and were beginning to specialize their focus along one of the triune paths: Teacher, Healer, and Warrior. Each was eager to impress on his friends the merits of his particular discipline. Of course they were all receiving training in the other two as well, so they understood the need and desirability of interdependence among the paths. There was much good-natured shouting, and mock dismay when an opposing view was expressed.

After some time, the talk became more unified in its focus, as each of the three disciplines was individually praised and appraised. It seemed the general consensus that of the three, the Warrior path was the most ambiguous in its focus. In both the Teaching and the Healing disciplines, the direction and application seemed clear and precise. Because of the Warrior's breadth of applicability, however, the attempts of the young men and women to define its perimeters had so far met with unsatisfactory success.

Their talk now turned to the subtleties of timing, and the appropriateness of the use of power in different situations. Again, the group found agreement fairly readily when discussing the Teacher and Healer paths, but harmony was more evasive in regards to the Warrior's power. Neither One-Who-Seeks nor the other Warrior students could resolve, to the satisfaction of the group, this question.

At this point, Singer-Of-Silences was seen approaching the students, and they all agreed to ask the Teacher to shed some light on their confusion. While not a Warrior-teacher—focusing, as he did, in the teaching of Teachers—Singer-Of-Silences was widely regarded as a great Warrior in his own right, and had given many guest demonstrations and lessons in the Warrior-training classes. So it was that as he came into their group, one of the young men asked him,

"How can we most clearly know when to be a Warrior?"

The Teacher paused before he replied, looking around at each of the assembled students, and smiled at One-Who-Seeks, and others that he had known for many years. Then he said,

"If you truly go the Warrior way, when are you not? If, on the other hand, you only seek the trappings of the art, you will never be. There is a common thought that a Warrior is one who wages war—a fighting man or woman. This is truth seen myopically.

"The true Warrior is the guardian of goodness, beauty, and truth. These three forces are expressed most clearly in an environment of peace and harmony. It is therefore the Warrior's duty, desire, and purpose to demonstrate by his or her every movement and expression the reverence for, and commitment to, life in all the radiance of its design. A Warrior wages war against darkness wherever and however it appears, by the sheer power and light of his example.

"Skill in the arts of fighting is a necessary part of Warrior training, but a skilled technician is not a Warrior. If you would be a Warrior, you must first release yourself from the limitations of the fighter within you. A fighter lives for confrontation and conflagration, for without them, he fears that he will be without identity and purpose. For him, the act is all.

"A Warrior lives to celebrate life. For him, the act is but a means to support that end. Knowing as he does that means and end are inseparable, he seeks to make every act as radiant as his goal. He approaches every moment with the thought that this act may be his final one; that this step may be the one that leads into wholeness.

"As the guardian of goodness, beauty, and truth, the Warrior overcomes by uplifting. If circumstances require it, he is the most highly trained and efficient fighting force alive. However, if he has been successful, violence need not reach its tragic end in physical expression. Sometimes it is so, but wherever he goes, whatever is given into his hands to do, the Warrior has it in him to transform darkness with triumphant light. And to do it all with joy."

# BOULDERS IN THE PATH

One-Who-Seeks came to his Teacher, Singer-Of-Silences, with a dilemma.

"There is an obstruction in my path that is holding me at an impasse, despite every attempt of mine to remove it or go around it. Can you tell me what I have done wrong, or what I must do next in order to proceed along my way?"

"What exactly have you done, One-Who-Seeks?"

"When I first saw it before me, I released a shower of Warrior-fire into its heart, thinking to dissolve the form, and consume its power to inhibit my progress. However, it withstood unchanged the full blast of my power.

"I then tried to move around it, but as I skirted its edge, it grew, so that no matter how far afield I traveled, it was there beside me— blocking any forward motion. I tried scaling its peak, and even digging under its base—to no avail. I know the path continues on the other side, but I am at a loss as to how to reach that point."

The Teacher smiled. "Let us have a look at this obstruction of yours."

In a short time, the two reached the place in the path One-Who-Seeks had described, and in the middle was a large boulder obstructing further travel. Turning to his student, Singer-Of-Silences said, "Watch closely, and follow me."

Then, walking up to the massive stone, the man stepped right through it, and emerged on the other side, One-Who-Seeks at his heels. Astonished, One-Who-Seeks stared first at the boulder, then at his Teacher, then at the boulder again.

Laughing, Singer-Of-Silences placed his hand on the other's shoulder and said,

"There are three kinds of boulders you are likely to meet in your journeys. It is well to know them all, as each has its own unique quality, and therefore requires unique tactics on your part, in order to pass.

"Boulders of illusion are not truly boulders at all. Their power lies in their ability to assume the *appearance* of the fact. *Believing* that appearance causes many people to allow illusion as much obstructing power as fact. However, in the face of direct Warrior-fire, these boulders quickly wither, and the traveler can once again be on his way.

"Boulders of sleep can sometimes offer a greater challenge than those of illusion. Resistant to being jarred awake by frontal assault of Warrior-fire, these will often harden in their resolve, and stand before force with surprising tenacity. They are much more responsive to subtle embraces, and can be easily surrounded, lifted, and removed, if approached from the side or back. This may require some patience of the traveler, but a small amount of time spent yields large satisfaction.

"Boulders of miscreation are perhaps the most challenging. Rising as they do out of our own creative power, they are intimately familiar with our styles of operating, and so can resist both direct attack and surreptitious enfoldment. However, implicit in their design is a doorway through which the traveler may pass, continuing unbound along the way that leads onward. The key here is impeccability. Within the power stance of his training, the seeker will always be able to find the door, open the lock, and move beyond this apparent stalemate.

"It is just such a boulder you have passed through today. As with all such obstructions, you will be responsible not only for moving beyond it, but also for removing it from the path. Boulders of miscreation offer little resistance to Warrior-fire once passed through, as you will see."

One-Who-Seeks again faced the boulder and released a flood of Warrior-fire into and all about its form. In moments, the stone that had presented such an insurmountable dilemma earlier was gone; and once again the path before him lay straight and clear to the horizon, and beyond.

# WOUNDS OF BODY, WOUNDS OF MIND

Joyous-Laughter-Gentle-Tears had been sent by the master Healer to a neighboring city on a training mission. The region had been having trouble with highway thieves that often left their victims dead as well as penniless, so to serve as her guide, and to insure her safe arrival and return, One-Who-Seeks had been chosen to accompany her.

The two young apprentices enjoyed the opportunity to travel together, for ever since they had first met, their mutual love for the journey, though it took them along different paths, had drawn them into a close friendship. So it was that as they went, they talked and laughed freely, allowing time to pass as easily as the distances beneath their feet. Soon they reached their destination without incident, and Joyous-Laughter-Gentle-Tears went in search of the Healer who was to be her supervisor in the place. One-Who-Seeks also went to find the local Warrior-teacher, a man well known for his ability in the art, and one the young student had wanted to meet for some time.

Several days passed, and in that time, One-Who-Seeks was able to observe for the first time as his friend went about her business, demonstrating the remarkable facility she possessed in the Healer's way. He had seen many skilled Healers, had studied the precepts of the art, and was beginning to appreciate its place among the paths of power. But until now, he had never seen it performed by a friend; and so for the first time his attention was undivided, and he marveled at what he saw.

The Warrior-apprentice realized he had always maintained in his mind that the Healer's path was somehow less powerful than the Warrior's—that it rose out of weakness, and therefore was in some way weak itself. In watching Joyous-Laughter-Gentle-Tears, however, he saw truly the power in the art; and saw that without it, he, the Warrior, would be quickly rendered immobile. He remembered Singer-Of-Silences' description of this way: "It is the ability to restore the ability to respond."

When he saw her again, after she had completed her work, One-Who-Seeks told Joyous-Laughter-Gentle-Tears of his experience, and thanked her. Laughing in the manner of her name, she thanked him as well, saying that he was showing her the sensitivity inherent in the Warrior's way—a sensitivity she had been inclined to deny.

Shortly after this, the two made ready their departure from the city to return home. They had traveled some distance when, as they rounded a curve in the road, they were ambushed by a highwayman in search of quick gain and small resistance. Caught by surprise, One-Who-Seeks recovered and drove the man off, but not before he sustained a severe wound. As he turned to reassure Joyous-Laughter-Gentle-Tears, he stumbled; and unable to move further, collapsed on the roadside.

Kneeling at his side, One-Who-Seeks' companion gently lifted his cloak, and found lodged between his ribs, a knife. Sooner than he had known, the Warrior-apprentice was in the debt of the Healer's art; and as Joyous-Laughter-Gentle-Tears began her work, he closed his eyes and silently lent her the support of all his power to restore his strength.

Laying her hands on the hilt of the knife, the girl then reached her Healer's hands into the damaged side; and as she slowly withdrew the blade, she closed the wound behind it, softly singing the Healer's

song that brings harmony into torn and traumatized form.

As her friend rested, Joyous-Laughter-Gentle-Tears spoke quietly.

"The highwayman's work is easily undone, One-Who-Seeks, for it is but a wound of flesh, and quick to heal. But the knife found its mark because there is an older, deeper wound of mind that has lain too long open—like a doorway inviting unwanted guests. Our attacker simply answered your invitation."

At this, One-Who-Seeks glared at his friend, but seeing that she was not chastising him, and was probably right in any case, he relaxed, and she continued.

"I will help you to heal this wound also, but it is you, my friend, who must do the major work. This will be a slower process, for it involves relearning how to move in an area you have shut off because of the pain. Sometime in that past you sustained a wound to the mind of your heart, and rather than healing that wound, you closed off your heart to keep it from further injury. But life, as you know, does not work that way. Form can only function given a healthy mind that insures an active and free-flowing Spirit. Your open wound has been an injury waiting for a companion. Today you gave it one. Let us then heal it also, so that tomorrow does not bring a more deadly visitor to your door."

Joyous-Laughter-Gentle-Tears began to sing again—the Healer's song that melts the veils of fear, and invokes the internal physician within the wounded. One-Who-Seeks felt himself gently bathed in the sound of her voice, and as the walls around his heart—that were like scar tissue around the wound— slid away, he saw the wound, and released Warrior-fire into it to cleanse and uplift it. After some time, Joyous-Laughter-Gentle-Tears laid her hand on One-Who-

Seeks, just above the wound, and said,

"It is enough for now. Do not tear away the walls, lest you tear more than walls. Let them rather melt away, and let the wound close gently. Now that you know it is there, you can protect it with your art as it heals. I will tend it from time to time, to see that all goes well."

They stayed there encamped for two more days, allowing One-Who-Seeks to more fully regain his strength. On the morning of the third day, as they resumed their journey homeward, he watched Joyous-Laughter-Gentle-Tears as she moved; realizing that he owed her his life; and more, that he loved her.

# GIVING AND RECEIVING

One-Who-Seeks and Singer-Of-Silences were walking in a garden, talking easily as friends. In the years they had known each other as student and Teacher, they had grown fond of their time spent together. This day, as they went, the older man watched and listened to his young pupil, and marveled once more at the process known as learning, that was really a game of giving and receiving unending joy for the serious player.

"With an ear to the sound," he thought, "all of life is a song that plays as well in the giving as in the receiving; for in truth, the two are one dance."

He thought of when he had first met One-Who-Seeks along such a garden path. Remembering all the lessons he had given the young aspirant, he smiled, for with each gift, he had also received; and so had himself traveled far in helping One-Who-Seeks along his journey.

After some time, the two came to a favorite place, where they paused to rest in the shade of a large tree. Silence also rested between them, and grew, as they listened in the stillness. Finally they rose, and as they moved away, One-Who-Seeks turned to his companion and said,

"With an ear to the sound, all of life is a song."

Both looked into the other's eyes, and then burst into laughter: laughter not of student, nor of Teacher, nor of any single thing. It was the laughter of life; the laughter of joy at being part of the whole; of being a player in the game of giving and receiving.

# A DANCE OF DREAMS

As his form lay sleeping, One-Who-Seeks rose, and ran unfettered in his dreams. He ran with joy for he was not alone: Joyous-Laughter-Gentle-Tears ran also, near to his side. Through the night they ran, and their running became a dance—beautiful, fleeting, intimate, enduring—a dance of dreams.

Nor were they alone. As they rose and fell, their steps became the dance between the paths of power. Warrior and Healer moved, and with the Teacher, merged as one great procession. Seekers all around them joined the dance, and as far as One-Who-Seeks could see, the earth was filled with the merriment and the laughter.

Then, singly and in pairs, the dancers emerged and moved to reach their separate journeys' end. This became a dance as well, though distant; its rhythms slow, and subtle to the ear. As they too went their way, One-Who-Seeks and Joyous-Laughter-Gentle-Tears found themselves in a meadow by a stream. Seated under a tree was a master, and it was he who spoke to them, and guided their learning of this deeper dance.

"Do not think dance is music and motion, if you hold these two in your ears and feet alone. Would you land with clumsy art within another's secret places, who move with grace and beauty upon this stony ground? Let all your living be reflective of the dance of life that flows within you, even now. Every leap of thought you take, every emotion you make, is a dance; and whether you stumble in ignorance or glide with understanding, it will be you, the dancers, who make the choice."

Here, the master began to teach them how to listen, for as he said,

"You must know the rhythm before you take the steps." One-Who-Seeks and Joyous-Laughter-Gentle-Tears opened their ears, and the deeper hearing of their mind, and as they listened, they heard: heard the tones and rhythms, the tempos and timbres within the dance of life. And as it rose within them, they saw their lives before them like partners waiting for the touch of invitation to follow to their lead.

Taking each other by the hand, they bowed to the master, and turned their journey homeward. As the sun's first rays fell upon his face, One-Who-Seeks awoke, the still-sleeping form of his beloved, Joyous-Laughter-Gentle-Tears, resting in his arms; and these words in his mind:

"Let all your living be reflective of the dance of life that flows within you, even now."

# THE LONGEST JOURNEY, THE FEWEST STEPS

"There was a man who lived his life traveling many roads to fulfill his needs, chase his dreams, and follow what stars sparkled brightest to his eye. Moving from one point to another, one step after the other, he traveled ever on, toward a goal he could not see."

Singer-Of-Silences was addressing a group of advanced students, including One-Who-Seeks.

"This man's chief burden, so he thought, was a hunger he could not assuage. He sought the finest foods in the finest and most far-flung places. He learned the secrets of every chef in the lands he passed through, and prepared feasts of unsurpassed quality and size; but the more he ate, the less satisfied he became. He sought the finest doctors, imploring them to treat his malady; but every night he went to sleep thinking he had found the cure, he woke up in the morning, ravenous. He traveled into hidden valleys and remote mountain villages in search of shamans and holy men who might know the secret that was the answer to his obsessive quest. Driving himself onward, he pursued his unknown goal that was 'out there . . . somewhere . . . waiting.' "

Smiling at the students before him, Singer-Of-Silences continued:

"You were not unlike this man when you first came upon the paths of power. You brought with you the imprint of the seeker: the need to fill an emptiness, and fulfill a purpose as yet unknown. This need led you to find your Teacher—your key to entering the ways of power. Ironically, the Teacher's role is to help reveal to you that which was within you all along. Hidden to your eyes looking outward, your 'fruit' lay waiting for you to look inward.

"That has been the focus of your training from the beginning: the lessons of balance and alignment, and the Art of Making Where You Are the Perfect Place To Be were means to demonstrate how to find that which you seek. Once you had found your axis to the Infinite, you had found the major key. The steps of the dance represented the various journeys you will make in learning and applying the power you earn. Just as all your individual journeys are one journey into wholeness, so the individual steps are variations on the theme of standing balanced and aligned within the structure of your axis, within the 'heavenly stance.'

"Now that you have begun the advanced levels of your apprentice journeys, it is important that you re-examine and experience the truth within the basic principles of the training that has taken you this far. When the potential that has lain ahead of you for so long is suddenly realizable fact, you drink a heady wine. Go back and master your foundation, so that your power, your control, and your expression have substance, and you do not stagger forward in a drunken manner, but move effortlessly, with pleasure.

"Do not lose heart at the number of journeys, and their companion steps, that still lie ahead of you. The longest journey you will make consumes the fewest steps of all those whose end you will ever seek. If you would find the Infinite, you need go no further than the nearest cell within your body. Why look some *where* else for that which is *every* where already?

"Remember this: the shortest route from where you are to what you seek is a straight line; and the straightest line is your axis to the Infinite. Therefore, seek first a heavenly stance, and you will find all of Heaven is at your feet, in your hands, and throughout the reaches of your dominion.

# THE PRICE OF FREEDOM

Singer-Of-Silences, Feet-Of-Mountains-Hands-Of-Cloud, and Ear-To-The-Infinite-Eye-To-The-Song were preparing their advanced students for the approaching time when the apprentices would put on the lighted robes of their chosen path, and move outward as Illuminati. There were three major tests, and their attendant lessons, remaining for the students to complete before they could take this next step on their journey. The three masters had met to discuss the tests, the students, and how best to assist in bringing the two together successfully. It was decided that each of the masters would be responsible for one of the three tests, and would meet with each of the students individually in presenting it to them.

So it was that One-Who-Seeks came to Singer-Of-Silences, and listened as the Teacher spoke.

"You are a seeker. For many years, you have taken that search along the paths of power. As you have learned, you have gained greater and greater power, and so, greater and greater freedom. And what does a seeker seek, if not freedom?

"The ability to explore, unbound, the way before him, with all its mysteries; the opportunity to pursue without limitations the indwelling sense of destiny that beckons him: this is a much-desired 'promised land,' and worthy of his finest effort. But what price, freedom? Receiving such a gift surely calls for a giving in like measure, lest the scales of balance be overturned.

"You stand within reach of levels of power that can bring levels of freedom only dreamed of until now. But before that power is given into your hands, you must prove that you are ready to receive it.

Therefore, I ask you, what *is* the price of freedom? And are you willing and able to pay? Do not speak now, One-Who-Seeks, but give yourself time to consider the questions and their answers' meaning carefully. When you have done so, come back, and I will listen to what you have learned."

One-Who-Seeks spent several days contemplating this, and traveled into the countryside alone in order to observe, without distraction, his origins, his movements, his directions. He listened to the voices of wisdom and understanding within him, and to those of desire and will. He allowed the young and the foolish to speak, and noted their opinions as carefully as he had the experienced. To every voice he lent an ear, and to all, gave his invitation. He was at a doorway in his journey, and he wanted all of him to pass through into the waiting adventure.

When he had listened fully, he withdrew still further within himself to evaluate all that had been spoken, and to make his decision. Finally, he emerged with the answers clear in his heart and mind, and then set out to find Singer-Of-Silences. He had not traveled far when the Teacher approached him, and smiled.

"I see that you have found your answers, One-Who-Seeks. It is well we met, for just as you are ready to speak, I am ready to listen."

At this the two continued along their way, and as they went, the younger man told his companion all that had transpired since their last meeting.

"It is true that I am a seeker," he began, "and that freedom is as vital to me as breath. The problem lies in knowing the meaning of 'seeker,' and that of 'freedom.'

"Some would say that freedom is the release from all responsibility. There are times when that state has great appeal; but without the ability to respond, what are we but victims and prisoners of fate? If there is freedom in this, it is the freedom of ignorance; surely not the freedom of effortless and limitless mobility that I yearn for. I will take the risk of being held responsible, since being so held gives *me* the choice of action. If mistakes and pain ensue, I at least will have the right to change. Otherwise, someone else will do the changing, and I will be left to manage as best I can. Where is the freedom in that?

"I have been told that 'seeker' implies 'lost,' 'dissatisfied,' and in many cases, 'selfish.' I have not found it so. It was only when I found your garden, followed you into the ways of power, and acknowledged myself as a seeker, that I released the power those adjectives had over me. Only then was I able to find my place; only then was I able to appease the hunger that drove me to your gate; only then was I able to look, and at the same time, live harmoniously as well.

"I know the price of freedom. It is this: with the ability to pursue any direction, comes the responsibility to remember why we are traveling. Freedom is not only 'from;' it is also 'to.' As freedom from limitations is achieved, freedom to express is released.

"My personal search is not an isolated event—I am part of a whole. No one else can sing the freedom that lies waiting for me; but my part cannot stand alone, and the whole cannot resound without the sound of all its parts singing. So when I find my freedom, I will not be leaving the paths that led me to it. I will continue along their ways, beckoning to those that follow. In this way, I will repay my debt."

Singer-Of-Silences clasped the young man warmly by the shoulders, and looking into his eyes said,

"You will have your freedom, One-Who-Seeks; and we will have our song."

# THE SHADOW OF FEAR

One-Who-Seeks sat before Feet-Of-Mountains-Hands-Of-Cloud, and waited to hear what the second test was to be. The master Warrior-teacher smiled at the young man, and began to explain what lay ahead.

"You have pursued your destiny along your path with diligence and art, One-Who-Seeks. I am delighted both in the destinations you have reached, and in the love for the journey you have displayed. As a Warrior-apprentice, it is particularly important that you look carefully to this next test in striving to move onward.

"As you have gained power, you have gained freedom from fear. It would not be difficult to say that you had eradicated fear entirely from your life. It would not be difficult, but it would not be accurate either. One of the most surprising, and sometimes frightening, realizations for a robe candidate is that in spite of all the power, knowledge, and understanding he has acquired, fear still exerts its force upon him from time to time.

"Fear is a shadow that lingers on the edges of light. When you step into new levels of power, you send the light of that power, and of your awareness, outward in a flooding stream. This scatters the shadow, leaving your movements clear of obstruction—free of fear. However, as you near the horizons of your experience, the shadows deepen, and you are separated from the unknown by an amorphous veil.

"You have come upon, and passed through, many such shadow-veils in your journeys. It is, in fact, the number of your successes that presents the potential problem. There is a tendency, as each shadow-veil is pierced with greater and greater ease, to say, 'There is no more fear.' This is a rigid and premature stance, begging to be overthrown. It is to reveal your stance, and correct it if necessary, that this test is designed.

"Fear, of itself, has no power. Its efficacy lies in its ability to render its victim powerless. This it does by performing as a distorted mirror—it reflects only the trembling and the twisted. Thus, if you are standing in your trembling and twisted members when you look into the shadows, it will indeed be confirmed to you that you *are* trembling and twisted, and that your fear is an insurmountable barrier. If, on the other hand, you stand in your strong and true members when faced with shadows, you will see that your trembling and twisted companions are in need of assistance; and you will then lend them support, and pass through the veil without effort.

"Here then is the test. You will take a journey, but without stepping beyond the walls of this room. It is along your inner pathways that you will be traveling, in search of what shadows you fear, and the light that will lead you through any darkness. I will be here also; waiting for your return, and a report of your findings."

One-Who-Seeks approached this test with eagerness, for as his Warrior-teacher had said, he was a seeker who loved the journey. Also, he was confident. He had heard the words, ". . . it would not be accurate . . .," but he had listened much more closely to, "It would not be difficult to say that you had eradicated fear entirely from your life." So it was, that as he turned within himself, and began to stride the internal highway, his step was light, and his mind at careless ease.

He had traveled some distance in this manner, when suddenly a jarring thought occurred to him. What if he should fail? What if he were found unworthy not only of his lighted robes, but of continuing in the ways of power at all? How could he face Feet-Of-Mountains-Hands-Of-Cloud after having left him so gaily confident? And what could he possible say to Singer-Of-Silences? This was staggering.

To avoid falling, One-Who-Seeks turned his mind to what possibilities lay ahead if he should succeed. But this was worse. Surely if *this* test was difficult, future ones would be even more so. What unthinkable things might he be asked—told—to do, once he had put on the robes he professed to want? Might he not be asked to endure levels of pain far beyond that of the "usual and the common"? Might he not even be told to die, in order to prove his understanding of the eternity of life?

The master had been right! "It would not be accurate." Fear was everywhere! How could he possibly face an unknown that stretched to infinity? What little he knew only confirmed the futility of attempting to ever know all that yawned before him. What might not be out there?! One-Who-Seeks was in crisis, and near to panic. But then, more softly, other words of Feet-Of-Mountains-Hands-Of-Cloud came to him:

"Fear is a shadow . . . a distorted mirror—it reflects only the trembling and the twisted . . . stand in your strong and true members . . ."

Slowly, carefully, One-Who-Seeks drew his scattering forces into organized formation. As his heart stilled, and his mind cleared, he saw the shadows about him; and found the light that would lead him through the darkness, back to the room, and his waiting Warrior-teacher. Opening his eyes, he saw Feet-Of-Mountains-Hands-Of-Cloud watching him with the same gentle, intent look that had become so familiar. Sitting silent for some time, One-Who-Seeks finally laughed, and told the other his experiences.

"My stance did require certain adjustments, as it turns out. Fear of failure, fear of success, fear of pain, fear of death, fear of fear —they all raised shadowy heads and distorted mirrors to block my progress. But truthfully, they all seem to be simply the children of fear of the unknown. That was the most overwhelming. Everywhere I turned, unknown seemed to wait. And not only unknown, but unknown maleficence. On the verge of panic, I heard your words, '. . . stand in your strong and true members . . .,' and that gave me the key that allowed me to find my light and my way home.

"If I may again borrow from something you once said to me long ago, it is the key to facing my fear: It is not the form (the volume) that counts. It is the stance within the volume of form I have that is important. In the face of the unknown, I must stand in the known —it is the light that will guide me. That which I have is all I need to succeed with that which I face—current volume matches current need.

"Infinity lies before me. It also lies behind, around, and within me. If, in time, I reach all of its horizons, *perhaps* I will be able to say, 'For me, there is no more fear.' In the meantime, I will be content to unfold a measure of the mystery as opportunities arise; and be thankful for the shadows of fear that lead me to the light."

# THE YOKE OF ARROGANCE

The third and final test was all that lay between One-Who-Seeks and his lighted robes. As he went in search of Ear-To-The-Infinite-Eye-To-The-Song, the young man thought of all the adventures he had passed through in his years of preparation, and those that still lay ahead, beckoning. He was in high spirits: excited, confident, proud. In a short time, he came to the rooms of the master Healer, and found him waiting inside.

"Come in, One-Who-Seeks, and welcome. I have been arranging your final test, and just sat down to wait your arrival. All is in readiness, so let us now proceed."

The master smiled warmly at his young friend. In the time since he had met the apprentice, Ear-To-the-Infinite-Eye-To-The-Song had often worked with him, and had seen him grow in understanding and in stature.

"I have not known you for a long period of time, One-Who-Seeks, but I think I have known you well. When Feet-Of-Mountains-Hands-Of-Cloud and I sent you on your first solo mission, to guide Joyous-Laughter-Gentle-Tears, we hoped that the strengths of each of you would help strengthen the weaknesses that were limiting both of you. The success of our project has been unequivocal."

At this, One-Who-Seeks blushed slightly, and laughed. The Healer continued,

"Your love for Joyous-Laughter-Gentle-Tears, and hers for you, is a delight to see, and the growth it has fostered warms my heart, and that of all your teachers. It also brings me to the subject of your third test.

"Part of the wonder in participating in a dance of two, is that it teaches how to move in unfamiliar areas of your own nature. You have broadened considerably, demonstrating greater sensitivity, as you have allowed your own feminine nature to be reassured and supported by the femininity of Joyous-Laughter-Gentle-Tears. This is vital growth: in order for you to move effectively as a lighted Warrior, you must be able to move both with dynamic, masculine power, and magnetic, feminine power. Half a Warrior will know only half success.

"However, not only must both the masculine and feminine powers be active, they must be balanced, and mutually supportive. Too often, they are competitive, and harbor arrogance and ill-will in relation to their partner. It is this arrogance that we are concerned with in this test.

"When you embark on a journey, you go under different circumstances than most men. With your gifts of power, you possess means for transforming the difficult and menial into effortless works of art. You possess superior power. Are you therefore superior yourself? There are voices within you that will say it is so. These are the voices that weave, and cause you to wear, the yoke of arrogance.

"This yoke is perhaps the single most devastating obstruction you will face in your journeys on the paths of power. It can bend an otherwise upright man, causing him to sag beneath the weight of self-importance; and blind him by turning his eyes only upon himself. Whether masculine against feminine, Initiate against unenlightened, or any one against another, arrogance is an insidious wound, for it instills a false confidence while draining true strength.

"This third test, then, will reveal to you the size and nature of the yoke you wear, and teach you how to remove it, now, and in the future, should you again come under its influence.

"I have said that your relationship with Joyous-Laughter-Gentle-Tears has allowed your own feminine nature to grow and strengthen. This is true. In order to achieve balance, we must now go to your masculine nature, free it of arrogance, and so free both powers to seek their harmonious tone. This will, in turn, free you to establish harmony between yourself and all of life.

"To do this, I am sending you on a journey of considerable distance to study with a remarkable Warrior. I know you have heard this master's name: Gentle-Hand-Holding-Sword is renowned wherever Illuminati gather. This journey and its test will be unlike any other you have undertaken, One-Who-Seeks, so watch closely, and proceed carefully. And remember this: appearance is only part of truth—Gentle-Hand-Holding-Sword will surprise you, but she is a master to the furthest reaches of her dominion."

The emotional shock of that single pronoun reverberated throughout One-Who-Seeks' mind. ". . . *she* is a master . . ." A female master Warrior! Of course he had known there were many among the Illuminati, but he had never before worked directly with one. A peculiar resentment rising into anger filled the young man, and he was about to protest the wisdom of such a test, when he saw the master Healer watching him closely, and smiling. Embarrassed, and angry with himself, One-Who-Seeks blushed deeply, and apologized to the man.

"There is no need for apology—it is your arrogance that we are seeking. It is precisely for this that we have chosen to ask Gentle-Hand-Holding-Sword for assistance. Simply by her feminine form she will be able to reveal more of your yoke to you than I. And she is a master at teaching aspirants how to lift these burdens, and to move beyond their limitations.

"It is the nature of the test to awaken sleeping monsters. Do not hesitate to let them rise, for it is then that you will see them clearly, and be able to choose your action accordingly. You are not here to prove you have no monsters—that you wear no yoke of arrogance; but to prove that you are able to slay or heal your monsters. Denial will gain you nothing but a more painful acknowledgment later."

Ear-To-The-Infinite-Eye-To-The-Song then gave instructions in how to find his colleague, Gentle-Hand-Holding-Sword. Reassured by the Healer's words, and eager to be traveling again, One-Who-Seeks bade the master good-bye, and promised to share with him the essence of the journey as soon as he returned.

For several days the young man pursued his goal, passing through many new and unfamiliar lands. As he went, he became aware of strange emotions and attitudes crowding in on his focused mind.

"You are a fool, One-Who-Seeks, to go along with such a silly 'test.' It is another example of how all this training—this so-called power training—is really turning you into an effeminate weakling." Other voices laughed with scorn at the passers-by and their puny attempts at life. "If they only knew what we know! But then, they probably wouldn't know what to do with the knowledge if they had it. Fools!"

The closer One-Who-Seeks got to his destination, the more active were these voices. He realized that these were the architects of the yoke of arrogance that Ear-To-The-Infinite-Eye-To-The-Song had described. He also realized that the yoke was larger and of greater substance than he had originally suspected.

Late one afternoon, he approached a small village in the region where Gentle-Hand-Holding-Sword lived. One-Who-Seeks was tired from his traveling, and irritable from listening to, while struggling to ignore, the insistant voices that had been nagging him. As he entered the village, he began looking for a well in order to quench his road-sharpened thirst. When at last he came into the central square, he saw before him something that turned his already cloudy mood dark. Several women stood gathered around the village well, drawing water for their evening work, and talking among themselves.

"Fool women, can't they . . ." It was as far as his thought progressed before One-Who-Seeks was struck by an unseen force that staggered him. One of the young women looked up and smiled at the stranger.

"You do us and yourself a discredit, One-Who-Seeks, to so casually and carelessly release the power of your thoughts on unsuspecting people. Fortunately, I was here to return that power to you before it did unmerited damage."

So it was that One-Who-Seeks met the master Warrior, Gentle-Hand-Holding-Sword. In the first days he spent with her, few words passed between them. It was unsettling for the young man to find a master so young, and seemingly so diminutive. But each time his thoughts lingered in this vein, their power was reflected back to him, and he spent much of his time dodging his own blows.

After several days of this, he grew tired of the bruising, and accustomed to the appearance of his teacher, and so his test—and learning—began in earnest. Gentle-Hand-Holding-Sword brought One-Who-Seeks to a training room which had a large circle drawn on the floor.

"We are here, One-Who-Seeks, to reveal the yoke of arrogance that rides on your shoulders. Do not bother to deny its existence, nor feel that you are flawed by nature because you wear it. It is an obstacle we all face. Once you begin to put on the garments of power, there will be voices within you that would twist these into the yoke of arrogance. It is how you choose to wear your garments, wield your power, and deal with your voices, that will determine your ultimate success. Listen now to your voices, and learn the ways of power that will lead you to triumph."

Stepping into the circle, and directing him to do so as well, she then told One-Who-Seeks to attack her with whatever means he chose to use. This form of training was not unfamiliar to the young man, but he was hesitant to assert his power against a much smaller opponent. But as Gentle-Hand-Holding-Sword stood waiting for him, a voice began to scream in his ear, rage filled him, and ran unchecked all about him.

Blind with anger, One-Who-Seeks charged the master Warrior, intent to rid himself of this challenge, this embarrassment to his superiority. But no matter how he thrust, no matter how much strength he called upon, he never laid a single blow on his opponent. Each advance was turned aside without effort; and finally he collapsed, exhausted.

The next day, Gentle-Hand-Holding-Sword again brought him into the training room, into the circle; and again told him to attack. This time One-Who-Seeks listened to a more disciplined group of his voices, and chose his strategies with greater care. But no matter how cleverly he attacked, he never reached his target.

On the third day, One-Who-Seeks took a different tack entirely.

Subtle and refined, he sought to overcome by undermining. Faced with a superior force, he postponed his actual attack until he felt he had eroded Gentle-Hand-Holding-Sword's power to a level equal or inferior to his own. But for all his preparation, the result was the same: the master stood easily at rest, untouched.

The fourth day found Gentle-Hand-Holding-Sword and One-Who-Seeks again within the circle.

"In the last three days, you have listened to many of your voices, One-Who-Seeks, and have seen that there is a great variety of them. However, all of the voices you have heard so far are yoke-weavers. Today, listen to the voices of wisdom and understanding, and allow them to govern your movements."

Thus saying, she invited him to begin. But from his first steps it became apparent to One-Who-Seeks that this was no combat. Inter-weaving advance and retreat, both apprentice and master moved together. The movements of the student were unspoken questions; the movements of the teacher, unspoken answers. Around the circle they moved, and in the dance, One-Who-Seeks was shown the nuances of power, and the nuances of darkness that would abuse power. When they finished, both bowed to the other, and Gentle-Hand-Holding-Sword spoke.

"Go now, and return to the master Healer. You have done well— lifting many veils, releasing many burdens. As you grow in stature and understanding within your power, you will find that the yoke becomes easy to bear, and one day drops off altogether. In the presence of true power there is no room for arrogance. From time to time, listen carefully to the voices that are weavers. Know their movements and their strengths. In this way, you will be able to manage your forces, rather than letting your forces manage you."

One-Who-Seeks returned home quickly. He was eager to speak with Ear-To-The-Infinite-Eye-To-The-Song, and to see once again his beloved, Joyous-Laughter-Gentle-Tears. When he sat before the master Healer, the older man listened carefully to One-Who-Seeks' account of his experiences.

"You were right in saying that this test would awaken sleeping monsters. And also that Gentle-Hand-Holding-Sword is a master Warrior throughout the reaches of her dominion. Between those two facts, I have learned much, and found that to a large extent, it was a learning of old truths at new levels.

"In the earliest days of our training, it was impressed on us that humility was an attitude vital to success. It was a difficult and rewarding lesson. In this test of the yoke, I have come to understand the meaning in that lesson. With the humility that comes of understanding, there is no room for either arrogance or a sense of worthlessness. Humility is not the absence of pride. It is the absence of denial.

"When we listen carefully, when we observe closely, we find there are miracles performed within us each day. How can we then be worthless? There are also miracles performed all about us each day. How can we then be arrogant? If we deny these miracles, we open ourselves to false prides, false phobias, false lives.

"Some would say that self-denial is a humble act. It is not. It is presuming to pass judgment on a creation seen poorly, and understood less. Humility is the willingness to listen, the willingness to observe, the willingness to release any perspective that is limited and fixed. Within that willingness is the ability to receive miraculous life. Within that humility is the power to remove the yoke of arrogance."

# A WARRIOR'S ROBES

Dawn came as quietly as it ever had, but for One-Who-Seeks, the day began with an audible sound and rose into a triumphant song. It was the final day in the festival of the Gathering of Season's Last Fruit: a day of high ceremony and celebration—a day like no other. On this day, One-Who-Seeks, Warrior-apprentice and seeker in the ways of power, was to receive the lighted robes of his path, and be acknowledged as a member of the Illuminati.

Joyous-Laughter-Gentle-Tears watched with loving understanding as the young man carefully prepared the garments he would wear in the robing ceremony. She had herself received her Healer's robes the previous season, and knew well the heightened sensitivity and the range of emotion that moved within her companion as he moved toward the event that had for so long beckoned and was soon to be embraced.

Looking up from his work, One-Who-Seeks' eyes filled with tears as they met those of his beloved. Touching him gently, she spoke:

"It is a thing of beauty that endings mark beginnings, is it not? Today you close an era that has seen you grow into a messenger, refined and strong. There is a sense of nostalgia in leaving the scenes of such awakening, and yet today you open an era as well—one that promises awakenings and growth beyond all that you have so far attained. It is well to look with fondness on your past, but better to look with joy into the future. Do not try to conceal your love for where you have been, One-Who-Seeks; but remember that it was all a means to reach where you are going. The celebration waits the honored guest—shall we go?"

In the Hall of Celebration, One-Who-Seeks and Joyous-Laughter-Gentle-Tears found their places among the assembled companions. When all were gathered, the ceremony began. Singer-Of-Silences, Feet-Of-Mountains-Hands-Of-Cloud, and Ear-To-The-Infinite-Eye-To-The-Song stood before the seekers, wearing the robes of power that marked them as guiding lights in a sea of brilliance.

The three masters first invited onto the dais those students who were ready to put on their apprentice cloak. As each received this token of past and tool for future growth, the masters and the observing audience paid tribute to them, and welcomed them into this new level of freedom and responsibility.

Finally it came time for the Robe Ceremony. Again the three masters beckoned to those waiting, and onto the dais came the robe candidates—those that sought and were ready to wear the Teacher, the Healer, or the Warrior robes of power.

One-Who-Seeks stood among this group, and in the stillness of the gathered hall, he stepped forward into his new life. Singer-Of-Silences placed the Warrior robes around his shoulders, and stood at his left side. Feet-Of-Mountains-Hands-Of-Cloud gave him the glittering Warrior sword that was the symbol of the art and the sign of the artist, and then took his place on the young man's right. Ear-To-the-Infinite-Eye-To-The-Song gave to One-Who-Seeks the long staff that was the mark of authority as a teacher within the path, and then stepped directly behind the Initiate.

Together the three masters raised their arms, and their robes shone like wings as they introduced this newest member of the Illuminati. One-Who-Seeks then raised his arms as well, and the light from the four robes filled the hall. Lifting his sword in his right hand and his staff in his left, the young man held both high over his head.

The fires of illumination flooded out of the heart of each, into the heart of all those assembled; on out into the heart of darkness that lay waiting beyond. Like a song of declaration, sword, staff, robes, and Warrior stood shining. One-Who-Seeks, Warrior and seeker in the ways of power, had made his Presence known.

# THE SONG

# THE JOURNEY

By the side of a gentle pool, in the center of a quiet garden, a young Warrior sat, part of the stillness. For three days One-Who-Seeks had waited, listening. The Illuminati, gathered to welcome him into their midst in the ceremony that crowned the Gathering of Season's Last Fruit, had departed. Alone he had come to the pool, alone in his secret place, to hear his first Warrior song.

His sword and staff lay at his side, his robes across his shoulders. These newly won symbols of his art he had earned in the years of his preparation. This first song, captured in his solitude, would reveal to him his first Warrior journey and how he would use his gifts in the years of his expression.

Out of the stillness, at the fringe of sound, One-Who-Seeks heard the first whisperings of the song. And then as it rose in a slow, graceful crescendo, he saw his way open before him. Rising in a single motion to his full height, he drew deeply of the breath of life, claimed his song, and began his journey.

Reaching to the farthest extension of his power, yet leaving not the least of his dominion untended, the young Warrior brought to focus the whole of his identity and purpose that he had come to know, and declared them before Heaven and earth.

One-Who-Seeks was eager to be on his way, but he knew there was still one task remaining for him to perform before he would be free to pursue his path. He must master doubt. This small adversary, so demure while at rest, so devastating while active, was familiar to him, and he did not wish to risk the danger of too casual a confidence.

Gently, he began to gather all the doubt within himself, and within his loved ones who watched his approaching departure, choosing to meet this subtle foe in his own time and place. Drawing his burden into the light of his illumined heart and mind, he related to all as to an honored guest. In this way, these "doubting I's" were allowed to see once again the true nature, design, and ability of One-Who-Seeks; and choose for themselves what to believe. Many who saw, believed in him. Some did not. But to every one, One-Who-Seeks gave thanks, releasing them from his embrace uplifted or disarmed, depending on their choice.

Freed of this last restraint, he swept his arms to the horizons, and seeing his way clear before him, turned from the place of his beginnings and was gone. The journey had begun.

* * *

As he stepped onto the path of adventure, the seeker remembered these words of his teachers:

"Never *fall* into a situation, committing yourself to an unknown. Place yourself. Acquaint yourself. Move yourself."

In this manner One-Who-Seeks now proceeded, so that as he turned and disappeared from the view of his beloved home, he went slowly, cooling the wings of his desire, and waiting until the direction of greatest wisdom should reveal itself.

It was well he did so, for even as he settled to wait, an advancing dark force came his way, and he was compelled to retreat. This is not to say that One-Who-Seeks turned and ran, or that he was afraid.

Was he not a Warrior of light? Were not these encounters with dark forces a very cornerstone of his purpose and design?

No, he retreated out of wisdom, and with power. Facing his shadowy adversary, he stepped slowly back, warding off intended blows, and sweeping his path clear of the confusion and debris dark forces often breed. Then, when the strength of the advance was nearly spent, he turned it aside, and sent a javelin of light into the heart of his opponent.

Drawing back the veil of his traveling cloak, One-Who-Seeks revealed to the dark forces the full radiance of his illumined nature, and sent a flood of power and light outward, infusing all before him.

With the radiance still upon him, he effortlessly gathered in his stunned adversary, and majestically turning in the direction he had retreated, carried all into the seat of his power.

Keeping stillness all about him, One-Who-Seeks now advanced, gently cradling his foe in alternating baths of regenerative strength, and emotional love and acceptance. In this way, he allowed them to release their wounds, and draw in the full essence of healing power. When he saw that they had awakened refreshed, he sent them on their way in a rush of fire that announced their transformation into pathfinders.

Watching them go, the young man drew his own forces inward to heal and regenerate, drinking fully of the essence of his work, and sending out a final gift of thanks and support to his departing comrades.

* * *

In the glow of triumphant victory, he became aware of what his teachers had refered to as the "pygmy I's." These were little voices that sat, monkey-like, on one's back; denying the magic of experience, and generally dampening the seeds of enthusiasm.

One-Who-Seeks wanted no part of it. But realizing how clever these little pests could be, he carefully devised a subtle strategy to loosen their hold on his shoulders, and silence their chatter. This is what he did.

Stepping slowly back as if to join them (which is what they wanted), he gently reached back with one hand to embrace the nearest pygmies; at the same time reaching forward to gather in the freeing power of the Warrior-fires he maintained throughout his dominion. Just when the pygmies thought he had finally agreed with them, he sent those in his back hand rushing forward into the fires, and drew more of the fire into his back to loosen the grip of those that remained. Working from side to side, he continued to gather in and push out, release and consume, until the pygmies and all their monkey business were gone. Resting in his power stance, One-Who-Seeks made it clear to them that he would harbor none of their shenanigans, now or later, although he suspected that they would try again.

Turning away, he sheathed his glistening Warrior sword. But then, in a rush of simple pride, the young man withdrew it once again and let its radiance soar upward and all about him, in a tribute and salutation to life, his teachers, and the Warrior art he loved so well.

It was now a quiet hour, and One-Who-Seeks could sense in the flow of his vital forces that it was time he tended to their needs. So, gathering the seeds of his generative power, he released these seeds into the space of his dominion, guiding their course that their yield might be most bountiful. This he did within both his masculine and feminine natures, for he knew that each must be refreshed and regenerated to achieve and express the balance and integrity that he sought.

Reaping the harvest of his loving care and tenderness, he brought the full abundance of his fruit into the Rooms of Assimilation, and shared with all in his dominion out of that abundance.

* * *

Fully rested, and eager to be once again on his way, the traveler wondered what new lesson would reveal itself. As he turned to scan the distance, there was before him a sight that at once answered his question, and drew compassion from his sensitive heart.

It was a broken man—not in form, judging from his size and apparent strength—but as the man moved, he nearly stumbled, for his identity lay shattered at his feet. He was living in emptiness, having lost his connection to life.

Calling upon all of the refinement and art he possessed, One-Who-Seeks reached out and invited the tragic figure into the warmth and healing power of an illumined heart and mind. As the man approached, One-Who-Seeks took him close to his breast, and holding him there, breathed life back into the shattered identity; and awakened in the man the knowledge of his own life-forces, and their magical properties of healing and revitalizing.

When the man revived, he told One-Who-Seeks the story of how he had come into such a state. It was a long story, so suffice it to say that he had, in fact, been a physician and Warrior himself. Because of careless judgment, he had been thrown into imbalance. This in turn had made him so distraught with guilt and shame that he had tried, convicted, and imprisoned himself in the lifeless form of living in which One-Who-Seeks had found him. Now, as he departed with the blessings of his benefactor, he took once more the vows of the lighted Warrior, and happily declared himself a renewed man.

One-Who-Seeks too was delighted. More and more he was coming to realize that the Warrior path was truly the Healer and Teacher path as well. Battles and confrontations were, at times, exhilarating; but the underlying purpose for it all, the awakening of life within all life-forms, needed the contribution and interdependence of all three—the triune path.

A second valuable lesson had also been given. From the example of the broken Warrior, he took new vigilance in maintaining the impeccability of his power stance within wisdom-love-good-will. And he also reaffirmed the need for compassion, and loving acceptance and forgiveness for his own limitations, as well as those in others.

The hour grew late, and One-Who-Seeks, stretching his arms to the horizons, saw in the moonlight that his path lay clear and straight. Spreading his traveling cloak like wings, and reaching his hands into the clouds, he stepped into that secret place Warriors know, when there is need for great distances, and little time to be traveled.

* * *

In this fashion, he soon reached his destination; and stilling his heart from the exhilaration of Warrior-speed, he once again scanned the horizon to see that all was as it should be.

Satisfied, he turned to face that which had beckoned him. It was a temple, and even though he had read much, and heard more in praise of its splendor, still he was awed by the spectacle before him.

Reverently he parted the veil and stepped through the gates of the vast inner sanctum. And here, as though he had been born with the knowledge, One-Who-Seeks began the steps of the Temple Dance—the greeting and salutation of the guardians and keepers of the shrine.

In the sinuous rise and sweep of hands, the explosive power and surge of feet, One-Who-Seeks rejoiced. And as he celebrated the beautiful temple and its dwellers, matching him movement to movement, the dwellers mirrored and celebrated the Temple Beautiful within him, so that a magnificent flow of love and gratitude, both giving and receiving, passed between the pilgrim and the powers of the sanctuary.

Then One-Who-Seeks moved into the Dance of the Lighted Way-Shower, gliding through the steps that were the vow of all Illuminati. In a clear voice that reverberated throughout the temple walls, he sang these words as he moved:

"Out of the Temple Beautiful, I will send my light.
Into the darkest byway, I will send my light.
The wounded and the lost, I will gather in.
The victor and the vanquished, I will gather in.
Into the Temple Beautiful, into the Holy Rooms,
I will bring the wanderers, the seekers after truth.
And when their cups again are filled,
Their eyes again can see,
I will send them on their way as beacons in the night.
Out of the Temple Beautiful, into the darkest night,
I will stand inviolate, a power of the light."

Finishing the dance, One-Who-Seeks turned and leaped in the Warrior's expression of joy-in-life, and then, facing the temple gates once more, stepped back for the parting salute to his hosts.

Standing first in his feminine nature, he expressed with flowing hands the love he felt for them. Then, drawing them into his heart, he gave freely and fully of his gifts.

Turning now to his masculine nature, One-Who-Seeks expressed his joy in learning the truths that had been given him, and demonstrated those truths with the power and strength that he promised to apply in all his Warrior journeys.

Preparing for a new and unfamiliar part of *this* journey, One-Who-Seeks gathered his forces close to his side, and moved away in the Warrior's walking power stance. Surveying the outlying reaches of his dominion, he advanced cautiously; remembering again his teachers' admonition not to *fall* into the unknown.

* * *

There was something here the he did not like, and stepping out deep and low, he drove shafts of light and Warrior-fire into the earth and surrounding area in order to clear the atmosphere and reveal the cause of his unease. Rising from his work, he searched the horizon for signs. And there, before him in the distance, was the answer.

Coming down upon him with the rush of wild horses was a mob gone berserk. Wreaking havoc on the countryside, leaving chaos in their wake, onward they came.

One-Who-Seeks, drawing on the very roots of his power, stepped into his full dynamic masculine nature, and strode into the face of mayhem. Parting the mob like waves before him, he hurled the vandals to right and left, into the Warrior-fires he maintained all about him, to lift the veils of fear and rage that blinded their eyes. Coming to the far side of their gathered forces, One-Who-Seeks paused to scan the horizon for stragglers. Then, moving into his feminine nature, he began to weave a vast net around the mob, anchoring it into the four corners of his dominion.

Now, reaching into the masses once more, he drew his captives into the still calm of his healing gardens, restoring balance and order, and awakening many to their own quiet places. Releasing them, uplifted and disarmed, One-Who-Seeks sent them on their way. Bringing his own forces back to center focus, he checked his bearing, and made sure his path was clear.

Not wanting to remain any longer in this inhospitable place, and sensing an urgency elsewhere, One-Who-Seeks again stepped into the secret Warrior-place, and reaching his hands into the clouds, traveled at Warrior-speed.

* * *

His next assignment was a special one, for he had been invited to speak to a group of young students concerning the way of the Warrior. Knowing that flexibility, both in body, and more difficultly, in attitude, was critical for the aspiring Warrior, One-Who-Seeks had devised a plan that would dramatically demonstrate to the students the need for cultivating this quality. Realizing that most new aspirants were drawn to the excitement and glory of the battle-Warrior, and particularly the powerful, masculine assault team leader, One-Who-Seeks chose to appear in a much different form; testing them for the flexibility of their concepts.

Thus, when he emerged from the secret place, from Warrior-speed, rather than using the formal approach and greeting, he sank very low and rose as if out of the sea. Immediately he began to advance toward the group of students like some fantastic bird, with high flowing steps and gentle hand motions—hardly the conquering hero.

Yet onward he came, and he held the students enthralled. In his unusual dance, he demonstrated a very high level of flexibility, balance, and alignment—which they all sought. And more subtly, as he advanced, One-Who-Seeks channeled a quiet, gentle, but very powerful energy and unspoken essence; so that meaning penetrated into their understanding, and they learned much.

Sensing that the students would benefit from hearing about his experiences with the monkey-like "pygmy I's," he demonstrated the technique he had used to repulse these nuisances that, left untended, could undermine the strength of the most powerful Warrior. He also took the time to demonstrate the use, and proper care and respect for the Warrior sword that they hoped someday to wield.

Finally, he admonished them to maintain health and well-being throughout their whole nature. It was only a healthy Warrior who could sustain the level of inner and outer flexibility that their art required. To this end, he taught them how to plant the seeds of their generative power throughout their dominion; tend the growing fruit; and reap the bountiful harvest. He taught them how to bring their fruits into the Rooms of Assimilation, and how to justly share their abundant yield.

With this done, as a parting gesture, One-Who-Seeks stepped into the powerful masculine nature that the students had expected initially, to further demonstrate the need for the Warrior to be able to move in several modes. In this stance, he now advanced toward the group, giving them the full floodtide of the energy/essence of their lesson; harnessing the currents of their doubt and fear within the twin forces of his enlightened heart and mind; and as a last salute, drew a pearl out of his heart of hearts and hurled it rocket-like into the atmosphere, showering its gifts upon their eager dominions.

One-Who-Seeks now stretched out his hands and turned his gaze to the distant horizon, ever-watchful in his traveling. Again a sense of urgency beckoned him, and he assumed Warrior-speed, in search of this latest adventure.

* * *

As time rested, and space flew by, One-Who-Seeks called upon his Warrior-lights to reveal the way before him. Vast dominions unfolded beneath his gaze, and as he watched he marveled at the infinite abundance and beauty of life that passed through the whole variety of life-forms. Then, far off to his left, he caught sight of something that turned his heart cold, and his eyes flashed with anger.

It was a group of young Warrior-students who, enamored with their fledgling power, had decided to impress some of the local people with their prowess. Accentuating wild threats with mild tricks and demonstrations, this small group had managed to confuse and terrorize the villagers into promising equally wild ransoms for their deliverance. What had begun as an ill-conceived joke had turned into a worse-executed reality; for the villagers did not understand that the students were only playing with them, and the students did not understand the ramifications of their actions.

One-Who-Seeks, however, did understand. Stepping out of Warrior-speed, and clearing his path before him, he turned to face the miscreant students with his full lighted Warrior robes ablaze.

He sent out a flood of commanding Warrior-fire that crossed the field before him like a wave. Stunned, the whole crowd turned and stared at the stranger. Wide-eyed and trembling, some of the students tried to run away, but reaching his hands high over his head, One-Who-Seeks drove the shaft of his staff deep into the earth, and held the whole assembly immobile by the sheer power of his stance.

In a voice that carried to all the students before him, he spoke.

"The gifts of power are too precious to be flaunted as toys for your entertainment. Not only have you abused these innocent people, you have abused the trust of your teachers, and the sanctity of the art that you profess to study.

"There is no greater sin for the Warrior than the gross negligence and misuse of the power that has been given into his hands to tend. You have demonstrated here that you are not able to assume the responsibility for even the minimal power you have. Therefore, as a teacher of the Warrior path, I now remove from you the apprentice cloak, and revoke the gifts of Warrior training you have received.

"The ways of power are a privilege, not a right. Until you have proven your willingness and ability to assume responsibility, and approach this art with the proper humility and reverence, you will have to pursue another path to your destination. Now go."

One-Who-Seeks then reached out to the villagers and apologized on behalf of all seekers for the outrageous behavior of the students. Drawing them into his heart and mind, he calmed their fears, and taught them how to use their own life-forces as means of defense and protection.

Within the group of villagers, he found two young people who he recognized would someday become great Warriors in their own right. These he directed to a Warrior-teacher who lived nearby. To all he gave his blessing, admonishing them to pursue whatever path they chose with love, wisdom, and goodwill.

One-Who-Seeks' journey was nearing its end, and knowing that his greatest task still lay ahead, he made ready to depart. Stretching out his arms, and surveying the distances, he waited for his way to reveal itself. A final time he raised the wings of his traveling cloak, reached into the clouds, and stepped into the Warrior-place, into Warrior-speed.

* * *

One-Who-Seeks had been chosen to build and illuminate a shrine, so that other seekers might have a guiding light and sanctuary to aid them in their journeys along the paths of power. As he neared the region in which he was to erect the structure, he knelt to the earth, and gathering up seven grains of sand, rose and cast the grains into the air, transforming them into seven radiant stars. From each of these stars, a ray of light penetrated deeply into the earth, forming the pillars of the sanctuary. Shimmering in the sunlight, these pillars rose in seven graceful archs to form a dome of exquisite beauty.

Performing the ritual Dance of Illumination, One-Who-Seeks acknowledged the three vortices of the triune path: the Teacher, the Healer, and the Warrior paths of power. Then, sending life and light outward in a gentle, powerful wave, he invited all seekers to come into the Hall of Celebration for the initial feast.

As the people approached, One-Who-Seeks welcomed and embraced them all in both his masculine and feminine natures, letting all experience the joy of entering into a loving place of peace and understanding.

When the hall was filled, One-Who-Seeks raised his hands high, invoking the power and light of Heaven. And as it came, he anchored it within every dimension of every dominion, of all those assembled.

Bowing to these, his beloved companions, he released into the hands of the chosen Teacher the keys to the gates of the shrine. And then, his journey completed, One-Who-Seeks returned to the quiet stillness of his garden pool, and waited the coming of a new day.

Photograph by Jim Chow

# AUTHOR'S NOTE

The stories and parables that make up these *Tales* are based on my experiences using the principles of Actualism  inner training, and Kuang Ping style Tai Chi Chuan outer training.

In 1973 I became a student of Actualism, and so began to travel in earnest the journey I had pursued intermittently for 22 years. I had always been deeply moved by my experiences of God. The reality of Spirit was never a question for me. My problem was that as I searched to learn and experience more, I continually ran into the walls of limited understanding —my own, and my teachers'.

However, in October of that year I entered training that did not simply reveal walls; it taught me how to remove or move beyond them. Actualism teaches not only the inherent goodness, beauty, and truth of life; it teaches the use of pure life-energy which has the ability to remove the walls and heal the separations between the radiance of the Actual Design and the conditions in which we find form.

It's difficult to acknowledge goodness, beauty, and truth when standing in an angry, bruised, and confused reality. However, with the proper tools, it's not difficult to soothe the anger, heal the bruises, and move from confusion into enlightenment. With these veils of distraction removed, clear-sightedness reveals life as it actually is—untainted by living as it's done.

That same December I was introduced to *Tales'* second major influence. I saw for the first time a demonstration of the ancient Chinese martial art, Tai Chi Chuan. Here was a system that taught physical motion to harmonize with inner music. I was captivated.

In the years since, as I have studied and taught Actualism and Tai Chi Chuan, it has been a constant and renewing wonder to observe the magic that is present in the healing process, the healing power, and the learning process that is engendered by true well-being. Walls of limited understanding still rise. But along with them comes the knowing needed to take the next step; not perhaps the whole journey, but the next step; which of course is the most important of any journey.

Colin Berg
Oceanside, California

Actualism, founded by Russell Paul Schofield, maintains several training centers in the U.S. Its headquarters are at 29928 Lilac Road, Valley Center, CA 92082.